TO
BRYAN

MANY SAFE

and EXCITING

ADVENTURES

SHIMMER

by

James Sorenson

PAGE PUBLISHING
Conneaut Lake, PA

First originally published by Page Publishing 2022

Illustration by Rachel Mckee

ISBN 978-1-6624-4668-9 (pbk)
ISBN 978-1-6624-4671-9 (hc)
ISBN 978-1-6624-4669-6 (digital)

Printed in the United States of America

Special thanks Rachel Mckee for the illustration

ACKNOWLEDGMENT

I would like to dedicate this book to my mother, Sharon Barnette. Without her unwavering love, support, and studious work, transferring my handwritten work into a marketable manuscript, none of this would've been possible. Not only is she one of the kindest, most generous people I've ever known; she is a ray of light to friends and strangers alike, always there to lend a helping hand or feed a hungry person. Her kindness knows no bounds. She is both loved and appreciated more than words could possibly relate.

Thank you, Mom. I love you.

A special thanks to Alex, my publicist. I appreciate your hard work and patience.

A note to all the light bearers of the world. Stay the path; fight injustice wherever it hides its ugly head. The road is long, and the path not always clear. But united we can bring love, peace, and unity. We will stomp out strife, injustice, poverty, and hunger forever.

Always love your mother.

CHAPTER 1

It was a cool autumn morning. The fallen leaves were blowing from north to south, which was quite common for this time of the year. The horizon was painted with splashes of yellow, red, orange, and brown. It laid out like a quilt on a ruffled bed, much the same fashion as Tobin's bed looked now.

He awoke in a splendid mood this morning even though he stayed up longer than he should have, especially considering the day that he and Tamara had planned last night. He had known Tamara since elementary school where she used to pull his hair and tease him because he was much smaller than her at the time. Then later during their junior high and high school years, they would often have conflicts running for class president and trying to outdo one another in grades and athletics. They would often have in-depth discussions about the ways of the Aztecs and their bloodlust to appease their gods. It was both fascinating and disturbing to see that a culture of people could snuff out the life of their own brothers to appease an invisible, uncaring deity. Often Tobin's grandfather, Shadow Hawk, would give counsel to the young tribal members. During one of such events, the question of how the Aztecs could be so ruthless to their own kind was expressed to him. Shadow Hawk explained that the decline and destruction of the Aztec empire was due to the fact that they lacked the mighty horse spirit. He explained that if the horse spirit had come to these people, "our people," the world would be a Utopian paradise. Mother Earth, "our home," would have been honored and all spirits would have lived together harmoniously. Tobin and Tamara made a pact that very night, that every horse that came to them to share its life spirit would be named after an Aztec deity in hopes of bringing peace and unity to their ancestors in the spirit world.

What started as a good disdain toward one another blossomed into mutual respect, admiration, and even an animal attraction for each other. This was kept under tight wraps considering the nature of their professional lives. You see, Tamara was a highfalutin attorney, always on the side of progress and the financial betterment of her people, the Havaka Mountain Tribe of the High Sierra Nevada Mountain range. Tobin, however, followed in the footsteps of his father and his father's father, going back to a time immemorial as a medicine man for the people. He was steeped in traditions and the history of his people and saw all too well the destruction wrought to his people from the progress of the White man. With their cities full of pollution, drugs, and disorder always consuming the resources of Mother Earth with no concern for the people or wildlife that will have to live with the dwindling resources and their lack of foresight for future generations to come. Yes, he was well aware of their ideas of progress.

However, today they were united under the pretense of adventure and discovery. They were journeying into uncharted territory for themselves, and the land was deemed sacred by the elders of eons. They called it a dreamland, as there had been claims that those who entered seldom returned and of those that did seldom returned with all their mental faculties intact. But these were rumors from an age long past.

From a personal standpoint, Tobin was extremely enchanted to explore this area as he could recount stories told by his grandfather, Shadow Hawk, also known as Grandpa Fred, that this area they were about to explore was where many enchanted and mystical experiences had been known to occur throughout the history of their people living in the mountains.

Tamara had her own agenda for wanting to explore this region. The logging and mining companies had both offered large sums of money to the tribe council for short-term leases of the land. The money she deemed necessary for improving the school system and building a modern health care facility on the reservation.

CHAPTER 2

The tribal council had been split on allowing Tobin and Tamara to enter the sacred land, but after the tribal leader, Light Heart's wife was diagnosed with cancer. The four-to-four deadlock between the council was swayed to a five-three vote in favor of a discovery expedition. It was no surprise that Tamara and Tobin were chosen as they were both respected in their community and couldn't be on further ends of the spectrum when it came to the leasing of the land. This, plus the fact that they were young, educated, and athletic, made them the obvious choice to chart the land, list the wildlife, and do an all-around discovery in the areas of leasing interest.

Their plan was simple enough. They were to meet at the stables at 5:00 a.m. Tamara was there early as Tobin knew she would be. So he took extra care to make it on time, as he was usually consistently late. She looked at him and smiled as he pulled alongside her SUV. She had the tail bed down and was going through her equipment as he came to a stop. He quickly exited his truck in an attempt to help her transfer the gear. "Good morning, Tobin," she said, and he replied, "Hello, Tamara, would you like a hand with your gear?"

"No, I've got this. How about you load the horses. They've been brushed and grained while I load the truck."

That was one quality that Tobin had truly come to admire in Tamara. She was always patient and one step ahead. As he walked to the stable to fetch their mounts, he couldn't help but notice that the horses were eating from fresh hay bales and the stalls were free from manure as well.

Apparently, she had been there for a while.

He found the mounts haltered and tethered to the side of the barn. Today, he'd be riding Camaxtli, and she'd be riding Atlauva.

Both were named after Aztec gods and carried traits from their names. For instance, Camaxtli stands for god of the hunt, war, fate, and fire. He is one of the four gods to create the earth. He is a large paint and would often bay at the sun and pine the earth. Both, powerful and fiery he lived up to his name. Atlauva is a beautiful sorrel at only sixteen hands, she isn't large in stature. She is both fast and graceful with a gate that is ideal as possible for an archer to fire at her prey. Atlauva stands for the god of water, archery, and fishing. Being that Tamara is an ace archer and loves being on the water the name was a natural fit. They moved so naturally together it was hard to tell where rider stopped and horse began.

By the time Tobin loaded the horses into the trailer and fastened the door, Tamara was warming herself in the cab of the truck. "All set?" Tobin asked.

"Anxiously awaiting," she replied.

With that said, he put the truck in drive and they headed out. Thanks to Tamara's early arrival and taking care of Tobin's morning chores, they got out of the stables a full half hour earlier than they had expected. Tobin thought to himself how much he admired Tamara's efficiency as he looked to see her staring out the window and wondered why he had never asked her out. She was single, beautiful, smart, vibrant, and athletic. Other than the fact that she was stubborn, opinionated, loved to argue, and basically stood on the polar opposite of the political and developmental interest, she was perfect.

"Tobin, look out!" she yelled.

He looked up just in time to see a huge elk standing in the center of the road. He swerved just in time to avoid hitting the giant creature. As he went to correct the truck, the horse trailer started to fishtail violently, pitching them to and fro. Along with the added weight of the horses, it was almost more than he could control. He swerved from side to side of the road, barely able to correct the sway. He gained control just in time to see an owl swoop a field mouse off the road in front of them. Pulling off to the side of the road, he asked Tamara if she was okay. "I'm okay. How are you? And where did he come from?" she asked.

CHAPTER 3

Tobin answered, "I'm fine. Let's check the horses."

They exited the truck and headed for the horses. Each checking their side of the vehicle and trailer as they approached the rear. Tobin announced that the truck and the horses looked no worse for wear and told Tamara to talk to their steeds while he lowered the trailer door so the horses could be checked for scrapes and cuts. First, he pulled out Atluava as she spooked easier than Camaxtli. He handed her to Tamara as he checked her over. After inspecting the mare, he deemed her shell-shocked but uninjured. Next, he tended to Camaxtli, his companion through many journeys. This muscular beast was fearless with Tobin on his back and the king of the corral. His noble companion appeared to be shaken but no worse for wear. The two of them walked the horses to calm their nerves as well as their own. Tobin was the first to speak, "Where did he come from? It's like he appeared from nowhere."

Tamara replied, "Oh, I don't know. I thought you saw him, but when I looked at you I saw you staring in my direction."

At this, Tobin blushed a beet red and tried to change the subject. "Well, I guess we should get back on the road. We've still got a forty-minute drive to the gated trailhead." So they reloaded the horses and headed off for their destination.

Tobin was the first to break the silence. "Are you planning to wear all three backpacks at the same time?"

"No, wise guy, but you can never be overprepared. It's better to have it and not need it than to need it and not have it!" she replied.

There is a logic in that statement that Tobin could not disagree with. Besides, he knew it would be futile to argue otherwise even though he was a big fan of packing light and traveling fast with speed

11

and efficiency. This was a joint venture and compromise was key to a successful outcome. "How about some radio?" he said as he turned it on. "I'd like to hear about the weather."

"What! Didn't you watch the news last night?" she asked.

"No. As a matter of fact, I didn't! I don't even own a television set!" he replied.

"You do realize this is the year 2020, don't you? You know satellites, smartphones, smart houses. Heck, they even have smart trash cans and litter boxes! You can't stop progress, Tobin, no matter how much you ignore it."

He replied, "Answer me this, Tamara. How come with all this technology, homes, and cat boxes are getting smarter, but people are just getting dumber?"

Tamara was laughing as she told Tobin, "You make a good point. Nevertheless, time stands still for no one! Not even you, Tobin."

Just as Tobin knew better than to argue a point with Tamara, she knew the same was true with him, so she just sat there, listening to the weatherman confirm what she had heard from the weather channel the night before—clear sailing for the next three days, not a cloud in sight or expected.

The paved road turned to gravel as they approached the mountain road to the high country. Ahead of them, they could see the road zigzagging up the side of the mountain. The road would take them from the valley floor at an elevation of sixty-five hundred feet to almost ninety-seven hundred feet, just three hundred feet short of the tree line. For trees above ten thousand feet, with the exception of an occasional spruce, conditions are just too harsh.

Tobin shifted the truck from two-wheel drive to four-wheel drive and they started climbing to the sacred land. His excitement, tinged with a bit of anxiety, for he felt there was an omen to be found in their close encounter on the road with the elk, the owl, and the mouse. In fact, he was sure of it. For elk are known to be ghosts of the forest, and sighting an owl was a rare encounter in itself, especially in the daylight hours. Owls are known to hunt at night and are usually retired to their hollow by the twilight hours. Yes. There was an omen here. He just needed to decipher it. He wanted to ask Tamara what she thought but feared she would ridicule him as superstitious. So he just reached over and turned the radio to his favorite rock station. Metallica, "For Whom the Bell Tolls" was playing.

To Tobin's surprise, Tamara reached over and turned the radio up, saying, "I love this song!" It was one of Tobin's favorite songs as well. Now he thought it a bit unnerving that this was the song that happened to be playing after their close encounter on the highway. Seeing Tamara air-beat the drums and lip-synch the lyrics helped ease his mind and brought a smile to his lips as he joined in with her.

They were quickly gaining altitude, and the road was getting rougher and narrower as they progressed steadily upward. To one side there was a sheer rock face, to the other an eight-hundred-foot drop to the valley floor. Tamara was visually unnerved as her knuckles were turning white from squeezing the "oh shit" bar. Tobin had to smile. He believed this was the first time he had seen Tamara scared. In fact, he was sure of it. It wasn't long before they reached the top of the switchbacks and left the danger zone behind them. Leaving the mountain pass, they were now in a meadow that had a slow flowing creek meandering through it. They had left all signs of civilization miles behind them, but here in the oddest of places was an airstrip and a hangar. The airstrip seemed pretty short for conventional air-craft, and at an elevation of nearly nine thousand feet, the air was quite thin to be landing small planes; nonetheless, here it was. "It seems so out of place," said Tamara. "Does anyone know why they built it?"

"Just a lot of rumors floating around, but no one really knows," he replied.

"Is it much further to the gate?" she asked.

"It's only a few more miles over that next ridge and around that bend," Tobin answered.

CHAPTER 4

They arrived at the gate at high noon. Tobin suggested that they loose the horses, hobble their feet, and let them eat fresh kudd while they ate a quick lunch themselves. By one o'clock, they had the horses saddled and were on their way.

There were no man-made trails in this sacred land of the Havaka, so Tamara and Tobin guided their horses alongside a babbling brook, on a game trail that was most likely made by deer and moose. Tobin knew this by their scat droppings. He was an avid bow hunter and an expert tracker. The combination of the horses' footfall and the babbling brook had Tobin's mind going back to their close call with the large bull elk, the owl, and the mouse.

Tamara was leading the way and turned around to talk to Tobin, but she could tell that he was miles away by the look in his eyes. She bent down to avoid a branch and had to shout at Tobin to break him out of his trance just in time to avoid the limb that nearly dehorsed him. "Welcome back, stranger," she said.

"Thanks for the heads-up," he replied.

"I was tempted to let you get dehorsed. Would you mind telling me your thoughts?" she asked.

At that moment, he stopped Camaxtli, dismounted and walked to the creek, bent down, and picked up a red-tailed hawk feather. Tamara turned Atlauva and faced him. The feather was flawless. The sunlight glistening on the amber red against the silky black, making it sparkle like a jewel. "A good omen," Tobin announced.

"It's a feather, Tobin! A pretty feather, but just a feather."

Tobin knew differently. "There are signs everywhere. Nothing is random. It's just a matter of determining the meanings of the signs. That's where you're wrong, Tamara. There's meaning in everything."

"I suppose you believe in the lucky rabbit's foot also," she said.

Just then, he pulled one from his saddle pack and dangled it in front of her. "As a matter of fact!"

She blew her bangs from in front of her eye as she puffed her lower lip and made it kink a touch to the left. The sight of her movement made Tobin's heart skip a beat. He had never seen her before in this light. He had always seen her professional side, wearing a suit or some kind of conservative dress. While she was a beauty in her professional attire, she was drop-dead gorgeous right now in riding jeans, chaps, tight blouse, and cowgirl hat on, sitting on her horse with the sun lighting her hair and making her eyes twinkle. He didn't notice it, but he was staring at her with the look of a curious puppy.

She noticed the starry-eyed look on his face and said, "Um-ah. Hello, is there something on my face?"

"Ah, ah well, I thought I saw a butterfly fluttering around your head."

CHAPTER 5

"It's a bit late in the season for butterflies, don't you think?"

"That's why I thought it so odd," Tobin stammered. She knew he was making it up as he went, and he knew it was a bad excuse even as it left his lips. It was far too late in the season for butterflies to be emerging from their cocoons.

Tobin mounted his horse and announced that he would take the lead from here on out. A slight breeze was rustling through the canyon causing the leaves of the aspen trees to fall and cascade down to the trail and creek bed. Tamara thought to herself that it looked like a thinner version of the yellow brick road from the Wizard of Oz as she imagined Dorothy in her ruby-red slippers followed by the Lion, the Tin Man, the Scarecrow, and the ever-faithful dog, Toto. As they made their way further up the canyon, the trees became browner, and the breeze increased to an occasional gust while the temperature steadily decreased. They had traveled around six miles since departing the truck. The days were growing shorter with the winter solstice quickly approaching. Both riders were aware that dusk was quickly coming. Returning to the truck and trailer would require riding in the dark on a game trail, which was not favorable to either of them.

Tamara was the first to speak on the matter. "It's going to get dark quickly seeing how we're in the basin of this canyon that runs south to north. Do you think we should camp or return to the truck and trailer?"

Tobin replied, "We've come about eight miles in the last three hours. If we head back toward the truck, we'll only get two or three miles in before dark sets in. I don't know about you, but a five-to-six-mile ride with only headlamps to guide us doesn't sound like a bargain. Let's find a clearing and camp there."

It wasn't much farther and they could see a small ridge. The trees were in the shape of a horseshoe with the U shape pointing south, perfect for blocking the slight headwind that was steadily dropping the temperature. "Looks like home for the evening," he said. They tethered the horses and Tamara set out to gather firewood while Tobin built a fire ring. Satisfied with the rock firepit, Tobin walked to the creek to try and catch some trout for dinner. By the time Tobin arrived back at the camp, Tamara had a roaring fire going in the firepit; her tent was erected; and she was sitting on a log, drinking hot coffee. "Hi, stranger. Where did you run off to?" she inquired.

Tobin produced the brook trout that he had fished from the creek by hand with a sense of achievement and pride. Catching trout by sleight of hand was not an easy skill to acquire. "Well, that was extremely thoughtful of you, but I already ate an MRE while you were gone."

"Well, doesn't that just figure. It probably came complete with hot apple pie!" he spouted.

"Lemon meringue, as a matter of fact. Would you like one? I brought enough for three nights of camping." Tamara already knew Tobin would turn her down—something about not honoring the fish that died for their nourishment or something like that. Besides, fresh trout sounded good, and camping always made her appetite grow.

Tobin went to Camaxtli and produced a sleeve of aluminum foil and a lemon from his saddle packs. He then proceeded to gather some fresh sage from a nearby bush. Carefully he sliced the lemon, placed it in the cleaned trout, and carefully wrapped each fish in the foil with the sage he had gathered. He placed them strategically in the open fire and flipped them occasionally. They smelled divine, and within forty minutes, he and Tamara were enjoying his fresh catch. Dusk turned quickly into night. Tobin went to his saddle and grabbed his bedroll. He took the time to clear a space of rocks and twigs and laid his bed rollout so it would catch the morning sunlight as soon as it cleared the ridge of the canyon above. Tamara waited for him to finish and said, "We could have shared the tent, you know."

"I prefer to sleep under the stars, and I didn't want to assume," he replied.

"Oh, rest assured, Tobin, I am very capable of defending my honor. My father was a military man and a third-degree black belt in jujitsu. He taught me everything he knows."

"Great, I'll keep that in mind if we're attacked by high-altitude ninjas! Besides, I don't think your karate will be useful against bears."

Tamara smiled. "No! But this will!" She produced a can of bear spray and said, "It works on people as well."

* * * *

Tobin revealed his .357 Magnum and with a smirk on his face said, "So does this."

"Men always so dramatic. Not trying to compensate for anything with that hand cannon, are we?"

"Wouldn't you like to know!"

"Don't be so sure, tough guy!" With that being said, she got up and went to her tent while he put some fresh logs on the fire. The breeze had died down and with it the chill that was in the air. The night sky was spectacularly lit by stars. They were so bright that Tobin felt that he could reach out and touch them. There was just a sliver of a waning moon to be seen rendering the forest and terrain around them almost pitch black. Tobin went to the horses and removed their saddle packs and saddles all the while talking to them like old friends and giving them a brushing. When he was done, he hobbled their feet and turned them free in the meadow just below their camp. Returning to his bedroll, he could hear Tamara rustling in her sleep. It was a long day for the two of them, and he was sleepy himself. He lay down, replaying the day's events in his head—the elk, the owl, and the mouse…the elk, the owl, and the mouse. Eventually, sleep overcame him.

He awoke to what he thought was the sound of thunder. The sound filled the canyon. Tamara charged out of her tent. The horses cried a loud fearful whiney as the sound grew louder and appeared to be rushing toward them. The horses whinnied again as Camaxtli and

Atlauva could be heard galloping off. Tobin knew at once that they had broken the leather straps of their loosely hobbled hooves. Tamara looked to Tobin with fear in her eyes. "What's happening?"

Tobin regained his senses, yelled, "It's a stampede!" and even as he said it, he knew it made no sense. For there were no cattle at this high altitude. The sound grew louder, and they could hear the beasts running under the ridge that they were camped on. Then as suddenly as it was heard, it disappeared.

"Where did they go?" Tamara wondered. "It sounded like they just vanished."

Tobin shook his head and answered, "I don't know. Did you ever see them? I couldn't tell you what they were. It was too loud to be deer or elk. Besides, this is too high to be a herd of cattle, and bison have been gone from these parts for hundreds of years."

The two of them went to check on the horses. Tobin was already well aware that the horses would be gone. They walked side by side with their flashlights sweeping the terrain. Tamara was the first to spot the leather straps Tobin had used to hobble the horses. The straps had been ripped in half by the strength of the horses' legs. "Well, our rides are gone!" announced Tamara.

Tobin, who was looking at the hoofprints, said, "It looks as if they headed towards the truck. Do you notice anything strange about the tracks?"

"Yes, there's only two of them," she replied.

"That's right, not only that there's no sign of other animals at all. No broken branches, no turned-up sod, no droppings, absolutely nothing!"

"That's impossible," exclaimed Tamara. "We both heard them! I nearly jumped out of my skin. I was so scared."

"I know. It's crazy, but there's no sign of other animals, period, let alone a stampede!" Tobin was puzzled.

"Well, what should we do?" asked Tamara.

"The way I figure it, it's one thirty in the morning right now, and we've got another four and a half hours till dawn and an hour after that till daylight warms the canyon. Our best bet is to try and get some rest. The day may shed some light on this mystery, and trying to track down the horses would be futile in the dark," Tobin mused.

They walked back to the fire in silence, each in their own thoughts, as the temperature steadily dropped, they could see a mist as they exhaled. Tobin stirred the coals in the fire and added some logs as he rekindled the flames. Once again, the trees were shimmering from the firelight, and sparks were leaping into the sky resembling fireflies on a warm summer night. The night sky was alive with twinkling stars and streaks of color from the aurora borealis that became more predominant each year with the thinning of the ozone layer and added pollution due to global warming. A shooting star shot across the night sky, then another and another until there were four or five at a time. Tobin took this as a good sign while Tamara knew it was simply a meteor shower.

CHAPTER 6

They sat, warming themselves by the fire, watching it in silence. Tamara walked to her tent and came back out with her bedroll and sleeping bag. She laid it next to Tobin's bedroll and said, "I think I'll sleep under the stars next to you if you don't mind."

"I'll enjoy the company," exclaimed Tobin. He then added more logs to the fire, and they both slid into their sleeping bags more for warmth than being tired. The two of them both keep trying to piece together the events of the night in their own mind. The rest of the evening was uneventful; nonetheless, neither of them slept that night.

Tamara was the first out of her bag and was busy making coffee and frying bacon. The aroma of the two items was just the incentive that Tobin needed to crawl out of his sleeping bag while stretching in the morning sun and grunting like a wolverine over its prey. Tamara thrust a cup of hot coffee into his hands as she said, "Good morning. Breakfast is served. Let's eat as we discuss our options. The way I see it, we've got two options. One is to return to the truck, fetch our horses, camp there for the night, and then ride bareback up here to camp for another night then return to the truck the next day. Option two is to continue our journey using this as a base camp, spending two more days and nights here, then performing option one. Which do you prefer?"

"More options and more coffee," Tobin replied as he handed Tamara his cup. "Options are something we're short on. Coffee is not."

As she filled his cup, she asked, "What do you think happened last night? I could swear it was a stampede. I mean the sound was deafening, but then there are no tracks, no broken branches, nothing

21

to support that scenario. Maybe it was an avalanche or thunderstorm or a sonic boom."

"I don't know, Tamara. Whatever it was, it scared our rides off, making our scouting and surveying that much more difficult. We're already eight miles into this canyon and it's widening as we progress forward. That combined with the large boulders we passed, which are glacial erratics, meaning that they were dropped off as the glacier melted tells us that this is a glacial-cut canyon."

"Thank you for the geology lesson, but I am well aware of all this. So what's your point?" she asked.

"My point is that this could have been an avalanche because the sound is amplified by the widening of the canyon. But I could swear that it was the sound of a stampede, only the evidence isn't there to support that! Camaxtli and Atlauva are gone. We've still got surveying to complete, and I need to make a topography of the area. The horses are a full day's journey to retrieve, and we'll lose two full days by returning to the truck. We know we have a four-day window of good weather, and I think we should take advantage of having our gear and provisions this high up. Camping any higher than this, this late in the season would be a bad idea anyway. There's no tree cover above ten thousand feet, and we'd be exposed to the elements. The temperature will be ten to twenty degrees cooler due to the lack of vegetation. That's my point!" Tobin explained.

"Point taken! So what do you suggest we do?" she asked.

"We climb, Tamara. You do have your gear do you not?" he inquired.

"I wouldn't leave home without it," she exclaimed.

"Well, there's a granite spire about two miles from here that has an elevation of 13,800 feet, the highest point around this area. It will make an excellent observation point and a perfect vantage point to topograph the land," he explained.

"I think you just want an excuse to climb that cliff," she stated.

"Yeah, there's that too. But so do you, don't you? It will be the first ascent. History in the making."

"Well, let's make some history then," she enthusiastically replied.

The two of them went to work on packing their climbing gear and a small number of provisions consisting mostly of energy bars and a couple of water canteens. When they were finished they set out on a game trail through a meadow that was alive with fall colors of yellow-, red-, and orange-turning leaves. It didn't take long for them to cover the two miles, and before they knew it, they were standing at the base of the large granite spire that loomed over them like a large rock castle.

CHAPTER 7

The sight of the enormous cliff face sent chills of excitement shooting through the veins of the two would-be climbers, giving them a burst of adrenaline. "Wow! It's awesome. How many pitches do you think it is, Tobin?"

"It looks like about 1,100 to 1,200 feet. That means it's probably going to be about fourteen to fifteen pitches. It's gorgeous polished granite. I mean it's solid rock so we won't have to be overly worried about brittle holds or falling rocks."

"How long do you think it will take us?" she asked.

"It all depends on how hard the climbing is and how difficult protection placement is. Standing here staring at it isn't getting us anywhere. Let's climb."

"Okay, big boy. I'm taking the lead."

"Wow, tigress, a little bit pushy aren't we. How about we flip-flop leads," Tobin said.

"Deal!" exclaimed Tamara, who was already ten feet up the rock, placing her first piece of protection. "Climbing," she yelled down to Tobin as she was moving with steady grace up the cliff face.

Tobin and Tamara had climbed together a couple of times in the past. Tobin knew her to be a very competent partner. She had the style and grace of a panther on the hunt. She was fluid and calculated. She could easily climb professional-grade routes, putting most climbers of the opposite sex to shame. Tamara knew Tobin to be an exuberant and dynamic climber who had established many of the hardest routes on the Owens River Gorge while she was off at college. She thought him to be reckless and crazy, often throwing caution to the wind. He would often run routes out placing only one or two pieces of protection. That meant if he were to fall, it would be a whipper of thirty to sixty feet, which could lead to death or a serious injury. Magically somehow, he always seemed to avoid. She thought that he had to have guardian angels watching over him, or if not, he was one lucky individual. Watching him climb was a nail-biting, hair-raising, gorgeous expression of what a human being was capable of!

Tamara had run about 120 feet of rope out and placed fourteen pieces of protection before finding a ledge to set a good belay station. The route they chose followed a lovely lie back crack that led to the arête of the rock. The granite was straight vertical and appeared to peel back to past vertical as the climb progressed. She set a nice pace for the climb on the first pitch, completing it under twelve minutes. She yelled down to Tobin, "Off belay."

Tobin flew up the first pitch, reaching Tamara with a boyish grin on his face. "That was beautiful. Nice lead, girl. Now let me show how the big boys do it!" Tobin shot past her like a lizard chasing a fly. It appeared as if he had suction cups on his hands and feet, sometimes leaping two or more feet for a solid handhold. He ran his pitch out placing only five pieces of protection for the 130 feet or so of rock he had climbed. He set his belay station and yelled, "Off belay!"

Tamara wasted no time climbing with the sureness of a billy goat. She passed Tobin, saying, "Show-off," as she went by him with a smirk of her own. Now being 250 feet off the valley floor, the trees started to look like bushes, and they could get a feel for how small we are in the grand scheme of things. The next three pitches were pretty straightforward and followed a perfect hand crack that left plenty of places for protection. The two climbers settled into a good rhythm as if they'd been climbing partners for years. Pitch six was Tobin's lead. It left the hand crack and went straight out to the arête, often making Tobin switch from the north to the south face. Protection was sparse on the arête, causing him to use his drill to set bolts as protection. This caused a slower pace of climbing, and he secretly hoped the three charged batteries he brought would be enough.

He intentionally placed fewer bolts, often running it out to fifteen to thirty feet between placements. This put Tamara's nerves on edge, but she said nothing. Knowing the reason between the long run-out sections, it still put her nerves on edge nonetheless.

CHAPTER 8

To add to her stress level, she could only see Tobin when he was climbing the north face. Tobin was forced to flip flop sides of the arête due to the lack of handholds on either side. The climbing had gotten more and more difficult the higher they got. Tobin could see a large roof section coming into view as he progressed up the rock face. He tried to pull himself up on the south side of the arête, but the rope became taut. He yelled down to Tamara for slack, but to his dismay, she yelled back, "That's it!" Tobin felt stress for the first time since they had started the climb. He was highly exposed out on the arête. The holds were sparse and intermittent. The climbing had gotten more and more difficult. He was in no position to set a belay station as the handhold for his right hand was no more than a nickel width and the left hand was no wider than a dime. Torn between trying to downclimb to his last piece of protection, which was a good fifteen feet below him, or taking a thirty-foot whipper, relying on his partner to save him. His arms were inflamed, and the thought of trying to downclimb all the way to the last bolt caused him to decide on the former. He yelled down to Tamara to "take!" thus letting her know to pull out all the slack and prepare to brace herself for the weight of his fall.

There was no slack as it was and she went to pull on the rope. Tobin, feeling the tug, released his hold on the rock face and went flying or in this case falling like a stone through the air. Tamara could now see Tobin falling. She had no idea how far he would be flying through the air as she couldn't see his bolt placement. Everything moved as if it was going in slow motion, Tobin's fall felt like it lasted an hour when in reality it only lasted for five or six seconds. They were climbing with dynamic ropes that were stretching with the weight of Tobin's body, allowing the friction of the drag on the rope to slow his swing into the rock. Tamara screamed up to Tobin, "Are you okay?"

Tobin yelled back, "Of course, thanks to you! I just wanted to make sure you were paying attention!" which was only partially true. He knew they would have to tackle the large roof that loomed overhead. Tobin yelled to Tamara, "On belay," and climbed up to the last bolt he had placed, the same one that had just saved him from falling to the valley floor. He anchored into it and drilled out a hole for another bolt.

He set up his belay station, yelling, "On belay," to Tamara; and she started her ascent toward him. Tobin was searching out a line on the roof as she climbed. Before he knew it, Tamara was standing by his side, staring with him. "Now that's a big roof!" she stated. "Looks to be about twenty feet to twenty-six feet or more long."

"Ya, that's pretty all inspiring isn't it? Do you see that big flake that runs like a lightning bolt to the left over there?" asked Tobin.

"Yes. Now how do we get from here to there?" she replied.

The rock face looked like a silver-and-gold granite countertop. The slab face was polished and appeared unclimbable. Tamara spoke first, "Let's make a deal. I'll lead the slab face, and you lead the roof." It's exactly what Tobin had hoped for, and he wasted no time saying, "It's a deal." Tobin knew where his strengths lie. Power climbing was much more suited for his style of ascent. Tamara, on the other hand, was much better suited for the delicate moves and balancing that the superthin handholds required. She would have to move her foot to her handhold, hoping it would hold due to the sheer lack of holds for both. This was where the gymnastic and ballet training of her youth would pay off. Gently she stepped out onto the rock face, each movement graceful and deliberate. Before she knew it, Tamara was already fifteen feet overhead and slightly off to the left of their belay station. She hadn't placed a single piece of protection.

This had Tobin's nerves on edge. "How's it going up there?" he inquired.

"It puts a new definition on the word *thin*."

"How about placing some protection, tigress?"

"Not many options yet," she replied.

"How about setting a bolt?" he asked.

"Look, I'm driving. So how about some silence from the peanut gallery!"

CHAPTER 9

Tobin was seasoned enough to know that placing bolts while lead climbing a slab was a sticky predicament. First off, it's a slab. Slabs were remnants from the ice age created and left behind as the huge ice glaciers cut through this land creating the valley that they were now in. Slabs were notorious for lacking places to put protection, often leaving bolts as the only option. They were at the mercy of finding good footholds to allow them to drill from. She was twenty-five feet into the climb before she took the time to set her first bolt. Tobin was relieved, for if she took a fall from before placement of the bolt, it would be a fifty-foot fall.

They were now almost nine hundred feet from the valley floor and totally exposed. She successfully got the bolt hole drilled and the bolt placed. She stood sprawled spread-eagle, balancing all her weight on her two footholds while holding onto a fingernail hold for her left hand. It was by sure grace of balance that she was able to perform such a feat. Tobin gasped in relief as she clipped herself in, now safe from taking a serious whipper. She was still sixty feet away from the base of the roof. This is where they intended to make their belay station for the ascent of the roof. Tobin couldn't help but admire Tamara's sleek curves, agility, and all-around determination in anything that she undertook. This was a perfect example of such an undertaking. She set only four bolts and one TCU for the entire eighty-five or more feet she had climbed and was now anchored in at the base of the roof. Tobin unclipped from the belay station and started up his climb. It was thin going, and he found the moves to be awkward. He was forming a new appreciation for Tamara's endurance and skills as a climber. It seemed like it took forever for him to get to the first bolt. He unclipped the quick draw and placed it on his harness. He turned to look at Tamara. As he did, she shimmered in and out of sight. The shock of it was just enough to distract his foot placement, and in a flash, he was falling through the air. The fall caught Tamara off guard. She had her hand with the rope in her right hand, thus causing the belay to lock the rope as Tobin fell.

The rope went taut, swinging Tobin down and to the left. Because of the long run-out between the bolts combined with the full weight of Tobin as he fell, this caused a large amount of upward pull directly on Tamara, pulling her up and slamming her into the roof where the belay station was anchored. The pain shot through her body, which made the rope temporarily slide through her hand, causing Tobin to start falling again. She quickly righted her error, but it caused her hand to receive some rope burn and scaring poor Tobin out of his wits. "Are you okay up there?" he asked.

"Yes. Yes. I'm sorry, I just hurt my shoulder a little," she replied. Actually it hurt a lot. She had dislocated her shoulder, and her hand burned considerably more than she was leading onto.

Tobin said, "I'm going to have to pull up the rope to get back to the rock."

Tamara winced as she heard that.

What Tobin needed to do was pull his weight upon the rope as high as possible then let go of the rope. Meanwhile, Tamara would get herself as close as she could to her belay point and rest all of her weight taut on the rope. When Tobin let go of the rope she would fall some of the distance that he would have pulled out of the rope. This process would gain Tobin about two feet at a time. With Tamara's rope-burnt hands, this would cause major discomfort for her, so she wrapped the rope around her upper leg to take the pressure off of her hand. This would help to dramatically reduce her pain. Tobin was impressed by her knowledge of the sport but was genuinely concerned about her injuries. Three hops and he was back on the rock. Tamara pulled herself back up to the belay station and anchored herself back in. Tobin climbed with a new vigor and was at her side in minutes. He pulled up the gear bag and set up a porta ledge so he could tend to her injuries. The first thing he said was "This is going to hurt!" and he set her shoulder.

CHAPTER 10

He was impressed that she barely winced. Next, he tended to her rope burn. He applied a second layer of skin bandages to the palm of her hands and climbing tape to her fingers. "That's so much better, Tobin. Thank you. That was a nice little whipper you took!" she said.

"Ya. Sorry about that. That was an impressive lead. Superthin. My footing just slipped and off I went," Tobin replied. He didn't want to mention that he watched her appear and disappear right before his eyes. He didn't want her thinking that he was going crazy. Besides, he wasn't sure what had happened and thought maybe his mind was playing tricks on him. Also, this was no time to have her doubt his ability physically or mentally. "How's your shoulder?" he inquired.

"It's sore, but I think I can finish. If my memory serves me right, after the roof there should only be one hundred or so feet to the top with two pitches max. On top of that, you haven't had the opportunity to draw your topo yet, and I would hate myself if I were the reason we didn't finish this route."

That was what Tobin was hoping to hear. Of course, he would have done whatever was best for his partner. After all that climbing, it would be a heartache to both of them not to complete it. Victory was so close that they could taste it. "All right," he said, "as long as you're sure you can continue."

"I'm sure. Let's send this thing!" she exclaimed. This woman had grit, and Tobin's appreciation of her was growing leaps and bounds. "Let's send this thing," he replied.

"On belay," announced Tamara.

Tobin grabbed and pulled on the lightning-shaped flake. "Seems solid enough," he said to himself as he set his first cam. Tobin was a bear when it came to power climbing. The flake was solid. It took his body weight without flexing or give, thus allowing him to show off a bit for Tamara. He had his legs down so his body was vertical, and to Tamara, it looked as if he was dancing across the sky. His showmanship was paying off in dividends as Tamara was duly impressed by his power, agility, and well-honed physic. Mutual admiration was growing between them. Tobin was nearing the end of the roof and had started using his feet toward the end because the holds were becoming steadily thinner and thinner. He had only placed two caming units for the first loft of the roof and had taken the time to place TCUs in the last twelve feet he had climbed. He was making the last move that would take him from the roof of the rock to the face of the rock, and it happened.

He started to shimmer, and then he just disappeared. Tamara blinked and rubbed her eyes. She didn't see Tobin falling to his death. She yelled out to him, "Tobin, Are you okay?" To her great satisfaction, he answered, "Ya, I'm fine." His voice sounded distant like an echo bouncing off the canyon walls. They were in a canyon, after all, she mused. Tamara was looking to where Tobin was just climbing and something was out of place. She followed the rope starting where it left her hand, continuing through the cams out to the TCUs, and there the rope just ended in the air as if cut by the ridge, holding itself up in the air. Tobin shouted, "Off belay," which meant he had the belay station set, but his voice sounded even further than before.

She wasted no time cleaning up the porta ledge and belay station. She yelled up to Tobin that she was on belay and ready to climb. The fact that the rope appeared to just disappear into thin air gave her no comfort. She thought to herself, "It's got to be shadows or something because the alternative is just impossible."

Tobin yelled down to her, "Climb on, hurry up! You've got to see this!"

She started her ascent of the roof. Her shoulder hurt, but as long as she kept her arm extended, it was bearable. Unlike Tobin, she kept her feet on the flake, either jamming her toes into it or using heel hooks to help support her body weight, relying on her agility rather than brute strength.

CHAPTER 11

The roof was amazingly fun with big jugs for handholds at the start with thin deep holds toward the end. Before she knew it, she was hooking her heel on the face of the rock and mantling herself upright once more. Within moments, she was clipping into the belay with Tobin as he smiled at her and said, "Nice job, tigress."

"Great lead. Now what's so urgent that you need me to see?" she asked.

"Look up," he said.

As she did so, she saw that there was at least another 350 feet to the top. Flat Top Rock didn't have a flat top at all. "That's odd," she said. "I thought we were almost finished and the flat top is actually a dome top! It must be some kind of natural phenomena that makes it appear flat from below."

"That's not all," announced Tobin. "Look at the meadow we drove through on our way here."

She turned her attention to the meadow. "Yes, it's beautiful. What about it?" she asked.

"Look at the road we drove through to get to the gate. It's gone."

She looked back once again and stated, "No, it's just hidden behind a ridge or trees or something."

"That could explain the road, but what about the airstrip and hangar?" he asked.

"It has to be a separate meadow. That's the only logical explanation," she countered.

"I suppose you're right," said Tobin, but he was quite certain that it wasn't.

"Let's finish this climb while we still have enough light for you to make your topographic map," Tamara urged.

The next three pitches went off without a hitch, and in no time at all, they were at the top of the rock. Tobin went to work immediately, pulling out his surveying equipment and charts. His work was masterful as he had done much of his work from his computer at home. His main goal was to get pictures, which he did in the dozens. "I think I'm done here," stated Tobin. "It's going to be dark soon, and we need to start our descent. I think we should trek down the low-angle slab to where it meets the tree line. If we get caught trying to repel the face, we could be in real trouble even with our head-lamps. The temperature is going to drop considerably when the sun drops behind the horizon."

Tamara was in complete agreement with Tobin.

The two of them packed their gear and made a hurried descent for the tree line. The only downside was that they were heading in the opposite direction of their base camp and were unprepared for a night stay away from there. Dusk was fast approaching, and a chill started to descend upon them like a fog in the San Francisco Bay area late in the season. The sun had fallen below the ridge of the mountains forty-five minutes earlier. They were making their way down by the light of their headlamps. The low-angle slab was steeper than it appeared, and it had taken longer than they had expected to reach the tree line. By the time they did, the temperature was in the twenties. There was a slight increase in temperature at the tree level, but it was still below freezing.

As they were making their way down through the trees, they came across a perfectly symmetrical patch of dirt that was well pro-tected from the wind by the trees. Tobin knew what it was at first glance, but the sight of it puzzled him. The two weary climbers both felt a pull to the opening. Seeing that there was a good supply of dead wood around and that the night was in full effect by then, they decided to make camp and began gathering firewood. Soon they were warming themselves by the fire. Tamara reached into her bag and produced two granola bars. She smiled and handed one to Tobin. "Thanks. Now if we only had some coffee." Tobin declared.

"Ask and ye shall receive," replied Tamara as she produced some instant coffee and a small tin pot.

"You never cease to amaze me, woman!" Tobin smiled.

"Thanks. I think you're pretty all right yourself, ace!" Tamara replied.

Tobin blushed as he filled the pot with water and placed it on the fire. Now that he was standing, he caught a glimpse of the moon above the treetops, and that uneasy feeling came creeping back in.

Tamara could see it in his eyes as he came to sit by her side. "What's wrong?" she asked.

CHAPTER 12

"What's right would be a better question. I just spotted the moon and it's a waxing moon while last night it was a waning moon," he stated.

"That's impossible," said Tamara.

"I know, but look for yourself," he told her.

She rose to scan the night sky and answered, "You're right, and that's not all. The constellations have all shifted too, representing spring and not fall."

"That's not all that's strange," said Tobin. "For instance, do you know what this clearing is made for?"

"No, I don't," she said.

"For tepees," he stated, "but it's been hundreds of years since our people roamed these mountains. This clearing should be over-grown by trees or brush or something. That is just the tip of the iceberg. There's last night, for instance, the sound of a stampede that spooked our horses off."

"Yes. But that could have been an echo coming from the canyon," Tamara said.

"Normally I could see the logic in that assumption. But in this case, with all the brush and trees, it's not possible for a stampede to occur in this canyon."

"What about a canyon higher up the mountain?" she asked.

"What about it? It's too late in the season for elk, and no rancher would be trying to graze his cattle at this altitude. Besides, there's plenty of green pasture throughout the valley floor," Tobin stated.

"There has to be some reasonable explanation," she said.

"What about the canyon with the disappearance of the road, of the airstrip, and the hangar?" he inquired.

"As I said, Tobin, it has to be a separate canyon!" she exclaimed.

Tobin replied, "Not likely. There's something else. I didn't want to mention it, but when I fell today I could swear you were there and a shimmer occurred around you. Then you disappeared and reappeared right before my eyes."

"How come you didn't mention that while we were climbing?" she asked.

Tobin got up and poured two cups of coffee from the small pot. Handing one to Tamara, he said, "Here, drink this. You're shivering, and your teeth are chattering."

She took the cup, saying, "Thank you. It's really cold up here. Now, why didn't you mention it?"

"I thought my eyes were playing tricks on me," he answered as he got up and started digging a trench.

"What are you doing?" asked Tamara.

"Making a heating blanket!" he said. He dug the trench seven inches deep and about three body widths wide and about six feet in length. He attached the empty pot to a stick and started to scoop the red-hot coals out of the fire and into the trench. Once he had scooped out enough, he spread it evenly throughout the trench. Then he began to pile the dirt evenly across the coals. Once he had finished, he took a branch, covered with pine needles, and raked the freshly piled dirt to a smooth surface, removing any rocks that would cause discomfort. He went to his pack and grabbed a thin silver solar sheet he had carried for emergencies such as this and laid it over the freshly packed dirt. He proceeded to put their backpacks at the uphill side of the solar sheet and laid the fabric that had been used for the porta ledge on top of it.

Tamara was secretly impressed by Tobin's survival skills.

He added more logs to the fire, stating, "It's been a long day, and time to get some rest. Let's plan on making it back to base camp shortly after dawn."

Tamara wasted no time getting into the makeshift bed he had created. She was surprised at how warm it was against the coldness of the night. Tobin climbed under the porta ledge top sheet and lay next to Tamara. The sky was amazingly clear without the light pollution of town. The sky was alive with the light of the stars, and the constellations stood out brightly with the stars as their backdrop. Tamara thanked Tobin for the warm bed he had created and instructed him to spoon her, saying for body heat, of course. He gladly accepted her plea and wrapped her petite body in his arms. She felt safe wrapped in his warm embrace. She once again asked Tobin why he hadn't mentioned her disappearing while they were climbing. He was enjoying the scent of her hair and the fact that she fit perfectly in his embrace as if they were pieces of a puzzle and she was the cornerstone of the puzzle. He told her that he thought that his eyes were playing tricks on him. Also, he didn't want her to think that he was losing his cool up there.

CHAPTER 13

There was some serious climbing to conquer, and the tending to her wounds took priority over crazy talk about disappearing, which everyone knows isn't possible. Tamara said, "That was a pretty first ascent, wasn't it?"

"Ya. It's a beautiful line, and other than my fall, we flashed it!" he answered.

She then told him, "Tobin, I saw something I can't describe either. As you were climbing that amazing roof, you shimmered and disappeared right at the crux of the pitch where you transitioned from the roof to the face."

"Let's discuss this in the morning. Right now we need our rest. What do you want to name our route?" he asked.

"How about Shimmer?" she replied.

"I like it. Shimmer it is then. Good night, Tamara. I'm glad you're here with me!" he stated.

"So am I, Tobin" she replied as she fell quickly asleep.

His mind wandered back to the incidents on the highway. He thought about the elk, the animal spirit of strength, nobility, pride, survival, and stamina. The owl symbolized a bad omen. It was a creature of the night and the supernatural. The mouse represented the importance of small, persistent action; the need to pay attention to small details; and how to discern the important from the irrelevant. These thoughts kept circling in his mind as he drifted off to sleep.

Tobin awoke to the smell of food cooking and Tamara stirring the coals in the fire. "That sure smells good. What have you got cooking?" he asked.

She replied "Well, when I woke up I heard the faint sound of a brook. So I went there to fill the canteens and clean the pot. When I got there, I found this brook trout trapped in a small pool, so I made a spear with my pocket knife and managed to spear him! Then on my way back I saw a bird's nest in a pine tree and thought, what the heck, I'll check it out. So I climbed up to it and found four little eggs in it. I think that they're either robin or blue jay eggs. Anyway, I grabbed them to cook with the fish and stumbled on some sagebrush, and voila, breakfast is served!"

Tobin said, "That's strange."

"What's strange? That I can cook or catch fish or fend for myself out here?" she angrily replied.

"No. Not that! The fact that you found eggs in a nest in the fall," he answered.

"I guess I was so happy to find them that it didn't dawn on me. But you're right, that is quite out of place, isn't it?" she inquired.

"Ya. But I'm famished. So let's take this as a good omen and eat! We'll think about that later," Tobin enthusiastically replied.

The two explorers ate with the hunger that only backcountry campers would know and savored every bite. They briefly discussed the events of the prior day and agreed on a plan of attack. They would follow the brook that Tamara had discovered as it led in the general direction of their base camp. They both could clearly see the knoll from where they were now standing in the canyon. The little brook that they were following was met by two more little brooks, and a crystal clear spring that was literally flowing out of the piece of granite they had climbed the day before.

The weather was pleasant with not a cloud in the sky. It had warmed considerably since they had gotten out from behind of Flat Top Rock. "Where's our tent, Tobin?" she asked.

"I don't know Tamara. We should be able to see it by now," he answered.

"Do you think someone or something stole it?" she inquired.

"I doubt that. It would be one thing if we left food in the tent, but our rations are tied off on a tree branch to avoid such a thing. The rest is placed in the fishnet and dropped into the stream to keep it cold," he replied.

"Well, where is it then?" she questioned.

"I don't know, Tamara. Let's wait till we reach the knoll. That should give us some clues as to the circumstances," he said. Tobin was already scanning the area to come up with a satisfactory answer.

CHAPTER 14

As they walked, they discussed the odd events of the prior day. Everything from the sound of the stampede that spooked their horses to the fact that Flat Top Rock wasn't flat at all. Along the way, Tobin continued to snap photographs with his camera and occasionally with his phone. He hadn't received a signal since they had left the truck. After a few hours of scrambling over rocks, they got to the valley floor which led to the base camp. "It won't be long now till we hit camp," he said.

"Thank goodness! I need a brush and some makeup," she anxiously stated.

"You don't need any makeup, Tamara. You're the most naturally beautiful woman I've ever seen," he said.

"You're too sweet, Tobin," she replied.

"I mean it," he said. "You are truly beautiful."

She blushed, and they walked on in silence. They started to round the bend that led to their camp, and Tobin thought to himself, "That's odd. We should be able to see the tent from here." Tamara was thinking the same thing. Tamara and Tobin were now standing on the knoll, and he was getting more confused because things were just not adding up.

Tamara was the first to speak. "What the hell's going on, Tobin?"

He didn't respond right away. He just went on scanning the ground, looking at the surrounding peaks and back down to the ground again. Then he took a stick from a nearby fire ring and stuck it vertically in the sand.

"What are you doing?" she asked.

"I'm checking the time using a sundial," he replied.

Tamara pulled out her phone and said, "It's eleven o'clock, silly."

"I'm not so sure that it is, Tamara."

"What are you talking about? It says it right here on my phone that it's eleven o'clock."

"That may be what it states on your phone, but according to the sundial and where the sun sits in the sky, it's only a little after nine," Tobin stated.

"That's crazy talk, Tobin. My phone doesn't lie. It's on a GPS satellite," she said.

"Do you have any signal?" he inquired.

"Well, no, I haven't had any since we left the truck," she answered.

"Neither have I. That's not all, Tamara. Look at the peaks. What do you see?" he asked.

"Well, snow of course, but it does look like there's more snow there than yesterday!" she replied.

"Now look at the knoll," he said.

"What about it?" she wondered.

"You see the firepit. Does it look different to you?" he asked.

"Well, now that you mention it, it does look out of place," Tamara said.

"That's because it is out of place. I set it up over here because the winds were blowing west to east, and I didn't want the sparks or smoke coming into the tent and look over here. This is where the tent was, but over here where this dead tree lies, there are two places where bedrolls were laid out plus a totally new firepit!" he exclaimed.

"Maybe we're on the wrong knoll," she said.

"No. This is the knoll. I'm sure I triangulated the site the night before, and this is it," he implored.

"Well, maybe the two who laid out their bedrolls took our tent," she thought out loud.

"I don't think that's it either," stated Tobin.

"What other explanation is there?" she asked.

"Normally I would use the theory of Occam's razor, but it doesn't fit here. First off, I can't find hide nor hair of our horses' tracks anywhere. There are tracks here, but they're bison tracks through the valley and the thickets," Tobin said.

"That's not possible," she stated.

Perplexed, Tobin answered, "I would agree, but that's what they are. Besides, there are two horse tracks here, but they're tracks of unshod horses. There are also people tracks here as well, both male and female wearing moccasins. To top it off, this creek is at crest level, and there's more snow on the peaks than yesterday."

"That's impossible," she said, shaking her head.

"I agree," said Tobin, "yet here it is, the sun, the mountains, and the creek all point to it."

"To what?" she asked.

"Not to what but to when. All the signs are pointing to spring," he stated.

"What about the bison tracks, Tobin?" she wondered aloud.

"I haven't the faintest idea! Do you remember the stories of people coming out of this valley with some of their marbles missing?" he asked.

"Yes, what about them?" she inquired.

"Well, maybe this is why," he answered.

CHAPTER 15

The two of them took a seat on the downed tree. They didn't say anything; both of them were lost in their own thoughts trying to figure out what was happening. It was a beautiful day with the temperature rising steadily while the sun rose over the mountain tops and they descended in altitude. An hour or so had passed, and simultaneously they looked to one another and decided to head to the truck. They walked side by side when possible and switched leads at times. The path that they followed was not the same one that they had come up on, but geographically it was the same valley. Of that, they were sure. The differences weren't subtle such as there were aspen trees where previously there had been none.

The main difference they noticed was that there were spring flowers everywhere. The birds were singing and displaying their colors as they did during mating season. Also, the butterflies and bees were busy pollinating the flowers. Tamara was the first to break the silence, exclaiming how beautiful it all was. Tobin was busy trying to wrap his mind around things while he looked for markings in the dirt and brush left by their horses. To his dismay, he found none. They were almost to the truck and trailer that were parked by the gate. He thought to himself that he was glad that he had left provisions in his toolbox. He was famished and knew Tamara was as well although she never complained because she was a trooper in the true fashion. As they topped the last knoll, their stomachs dropped. Not only was the truck gone but the gate and the road were no longer there either.

"That's not possible," stated Tobin. "I know for certain that this was the place we left from."

Tamara knew it as well. "It's definitely over there that we parked the truck and trailer. I'm certain of it. I remember that huge rock over there" she remarked.

"It's called a glacial erratic," Tobin said.

"I don't care what you call it, Santa Claus, the Easter Bunny, or Mary Poppins. That rock was on the passenger side of the truck when we parked here three days ago! Parked where? There isn't a road, a gate, or any sign of civilization anywhere!" she exclaimed.

The two of them tried to rationalize their situation. The problem was that there was nothing to rationalize over. They were clearly in the right spot, but the situation was all wrong. After some deliberation, they decided that they should head for the airstrip and the hangar. It was only a short hike to it from their current location. After half an hour of hiking, they were at the top of the knoll where they could see the meadow below, and what they saw astonished them. The airstrip and hangar were nowhere to be seen. Instead, the meadow was full of bison. There must have been hundreds if not thousands of them grazing in the fertile meadow. The two of them stood there, frozen in their tracks.

It had been at least a hundred years since the White man had hunted these majestic animals to near extinction. They could hardly believe their eyes. Their other senses seemed to be tricking them as well. The sky and the scenery seemed brighter, the air crisper, and they could hear the wildlife with a certain clarity that they had not known before. The day had grown long and they were both weary with mental shock and a lack of nutrition. They decided to erect camp right where they were. This was a simple process as they had no tent to put up, few supplies, no rations, and their canteens were running low. Tobin removed his .357 from his climbing pack, grabbed both canteens, and headed back toward the stream.

Tamara asked him where he was going without her.

He told her, "I thought you might be too tired and want to rest."

She replied, "Not that tired. Besides, you aren't going anywhere without me till we figure out what the hell is going on here!"

CHAPTER 16

They both fell silent on their way back to the creek, lost in their own thoughts. Suddenly Tobin spotted something out of the corner of his eye. It was a deer getting a drink from the creek. He motioned for Tamara to stop, putting his index finger to his lips with one arm while motioning to get low with the other. They were downwind of the deer, and it hadn't been alerted to their presence yet. Tobin pointed toward the deer and made an eating gesture with his hands. Tamara's first reaction was to shake her head no. She couldn't bear the thought of harming such a majestic animal. Tobin whispered that they had to eat and their rations were about nil. Tamara contemplated what he had said and then nodded her head yes in agreement.

Tobin pointed to a boulder about thirty yards downstream from their current location. He told Tamara to hold up until he reached the boulder. At that time she was to slowly make her way upstream from where the deer was drinking. He figured the deer would head downstream away from the scent of the human intruder. He was right. The doe picked up her head and perked up her ears after catching the scent of Tamara. Tobin knew instinctively that he would only have one shot at killing his quarry. Since he had a pistol other than a rifle, he would have to get within a hundred feet or less to make an accurate shot.

To his delight, the doe headed directly toward him. It ran at a good click, staying between the boulder that hid Tobin and the creek from which it drank. The distance between the two was no more than fifty feet apart. Tobin aimed, waiting for a perfect shot, and gently squeezed the trigger. *Boom*, the larger caliber pistol jumped in his hand while the noise of the shot echoed throughout the valley. The deer made one last jump and came to a dead halt only five feet away from where he stood. It was a perfect shot right through the heart.

Tamara came running to where Tobin stood, screaming, "Well done, cowboy!"

"I'm Indian, remember?" he said.

"Oh come on, you know what I meant!" she replied.

"Ya. I was just poking fun at you," he told her.

Tamara approached Tobin, who was hovering over the deer, as she stifled back a tear when he produced a knife and removed the heart. He took a bite and handed it to her. She shook her head no and said, "No way!" Tobin replied that it was honoring the spirit of the deer who had just given its life so they wouldn't lose theirs. Tamara grimaced as she took the heart from Tobin's hand. The heart was warm in her hand, and when she took a bite, bright-red blood dribbled down her chin. Then they both raised the heart to the sky and offered up thanks and praise to the Sky Father.

Tobin field dressed the deer while Tamara filled the canteens at the creek. They made camp that night at the base of the knoll. Their campfire snapped and crackled as it illuminated the area around the camp, casting shadows that made them appear as giants against the backdrop of the knoll. Tamara was entertaining herself by making shadow animals while Tobin was busy making a rotisserie and an oven for smoking and cooking the deer. Off in the distance, a lone coyote started to yip. They looked out to the meadow, and there were bison from one end to the other. Some slept lying down while others slept standing up. It was an unseasonably warm evening as the two of them ate in relative silence, gazing at the star-filled sky.

Tamara dozed off first, allowing Tobin to study her in the light of the dancing fire. He stood up and added a log to the fire. Then he covered her with his windbreaker. After tending to the deer meat in the smoker he had made, he decided to walk the perimeter of their camp. When he returned, he lay down by Tamara's side.

CHAPTER 17

He was in awe of how she was handling the situation. Heck, for that matter, he didn't know how else they could be handling their situation. He lay down, and sleep overcame him. He awakened with Tamara shaking him violently, telling him to wake up. When he tried to sit up, she held him down, saying, "Listen!" He thought he could hear drumming in the distance and then it was almost on top of them.

A wolf started to howl. The howl was returned by other wolves that weren't too far off in the distance. Tobin thought to himself there haven't been wolf packs in this area for centuries. Then another howl made him realize that they were getting closer and that they were being attracted by the smell of the smoking meat. He looked for his backpack and saw it leaning against a tree over twelve feet away. "Shit," he said under his breath. He needed his gun. He had let his guard down and was now paying the price. Tamara pointed out into the dark. He followed the direction of her finger and saw two glowing green eyes staring back at him. He looked to his left then to his right and saw four more sets of eyes staring back. Not good. Not good at all! The gun was twelve feet away, buried in his pack. The fire was two feet away, and his knife was by his side. He reached for a burning branch that was half consumed by fire.

The closest wolf jumped! He jabbed at it with his fiery stick as the wolf bared its fangs and darted to the side. Tamara followed his lead, and the two stood back to back fighting off the pack. The fire was losing its effect on their attackers. Tobin knew that once the flames died, it would be over for them. He needed to do something and do it quickly. Then it hit him like a bolt of lightning. He grabbed his hunting knife from its sheath and dove for the base of the tree where he had hung the deer to dress it. He swung his knife as if it were a samurai sword. With one swipe, he severed the rope that held the deer carcass. The deer hit the ground with a thud. The pack immediately diverted their attention from the humans to the deer. The alpha male quickly claimed the prize and dragged the deer off into the darkness.

Tamara broke out into tears and stated, "I've never been so scared in my life! Do you think they're gone?"

Tobin took her by the hand and led her to the fire. He stoked it with fresh fuel and sat next to her rubbing her head as she cried on his shoulder. He said, "Yes, they're gone. We'll be okay now." Then he stood, retrieved his revolver from his pack, and sat by her side. "We'll be fine. I promise I won't let anything happen to you." Even as he said it, he knew it to be true. He would indeed lose his own life to protect hers in this strange and unfamiliar place. It was her that was helping him keep his sanity and if for nothing else, someone to be strong for. Within an hour she was asleep in his arms. He would not sleep this night. It was not until dawn that he finally rested his eyes, having fought off sleep for as long as he could. Exhaustion and stress eventually took their toll.

The position of the sun indicated that it was roughly 9:00 a.m. Tamara was shaking him awake gently at the start but became more panicked as Tobin opened his groggy eyes. "What time is it?" he asked. She pursed her lips together and brought her finger to them, shushing him as he spoke. With her other hand, she pointed eastward. He followed the line of her hand and saw three riders on their mounts. The figures were blurred because the bright sun shone directly behind them. At first, he thought his eyes were failing him; but as he focused on, the riders he realized they were not. In front of him sat the three noblest-looking Indians he had ever seen. They were speaking in the ancient tongue, of that he was sure. His grandfather had often talked to him in this manner as a child. It had been the better part of two decades since he had heard this spoken word. The riders sat talking among themselves; he could make out only parts of what they were saying. Tamara looked to Tobin quizzically and asked if he could make out what they were saying.

CHAPTER 18

They were speaking rapidly, and he could only make out a few words. "They are trying to figure out what we are," he replied.

"That's ridiculous. We're humans just like them," she said. She tried to raise herself to speak with them, but Tobin stopped her. Nonetheless, her sudden movement startled their onlookers, and two of the three warriors quickly quivered an arrow in their bow and pointed it at her. The third warrior ordered them to halt before they could set loose their arrows.

Sweat dripped from Tobin's forehead as he told Tamara to be very still and very quiet. "Don't move so much as a muscle. As I said, they're trying to figure out what we are." The leader of the party seemed to be eyeing Tobin's haltered revolver that lay on his hip. "They seem to think that we're Skywalkers from what I can make out," he said to Tamara.

"What's a Skywalker?" she asked.

"I have no idea," replied Tobin.

The same Indian that had stopped the warriors setting loose their arrows looked to the sky. He pointed up and looked toward Tobin. In the ancient language, he asked Tobin, "Do you come from the sky?"

Tobin understood his words although they came out slower and with more body gestures. He answered in the ancient tongue and told him, "We come from the earth just as you."

The leader of the three stared at Tobin, speechless. He didn't expect to hear their tribe's speech coming from this foreigner. His two comrades started speaking with hushed tones.

Tobin was only able to catch a small part of the words they were saying. He relayed what he could make out to Tamara. "They heard my gunshot when we killed our dinner last night. Their chief is the one who is speaking to us. They came this way to find out whether the cause was thunder or something else."

"We're the cause. Tell them it's us," said Tamara.

"Not so fast, Tamara. That's our only safety net, and I don't want to expose our hand too early. We're at a disadvantage here. One other thing, do not speak to them. It is not customary to let the woman speak for the men. It is a grave disrespect to me if I let you speak for us," Tobin explained.

"That's ridiculous. This is the year 2020, and women's suffrage ended years ago!" she huffed.

"Look around Tamara, this isn't 2020. We're not in our time zone, let alone our time period. Somehow we've traveled back in time!" Tobin exclaimed.

The chief was done talking. He dismounted his horse and approached Tobin, asking, "Did you hear thunder yesterday when it was late in the day?"

"No. Although I did hear a loud booming sound," Tobin replied as he pointed toward the cliffs, "it must have been a rockslide."

The chief knew what they had heard was no rockslide; nonetheless, he played along as his attention was diverted to their attire. He had never seen the likes of the colored animal skins that these foreigners were wearing. He was trying to ask Tobin where the brightly colored animals were that produced such colorful skins, but Tobin did not understand the chief but knew he was talking about their clothing. He decided to remove his jacket and present it as a gift to the chief. The chief took this as a great honor and removed his decorative chest plate and handed it to Tobin, who thanked the chief in his own tongue.

They engaged in conversation, and Tobin was surprised at the recollection of his native tongue. After all, it was his grandfather who talked to him in his native speech, and that was nearly fourteen years ago. Tobin was only nine years old when his grandfather had moved on to the spirit world. His father had vanished when he was only eight, and his mother would rarely speak of him. From what Tobin remembered, his father was a behemoth of a man who had been held in much admiration throughout his tribe and the tribal nation council.

Tamara waited patiently as the men spoke catching small snippets of their conversation. It seemed as if there would be no end to their banter. Tobin looked at Tamara and said, "We've been invited to their village as esteemed guests of the chief."

CHAPTER 19

"Oh, by the way, they think you're my wife, and it seemed the right thing to let them believe that considering how difficult it would be to explain the dynamics of our circumstances."

Tamara looked at Tobin with a distressed look on her face.

"Does the thought of you being my wife appall you?" he asked.

"Not at all. Actually, I'm flattered by the thought," she answered, causing Tobin to blush.

Tamara and Tobin secured their backpacks and climbed upon a small boulder as the chief had directed them to. Then the two warriors pulled up next to them, allowing them to mount the horses. They held onto the backs of the warriors as they rode off. They headed southeast, much the same direction that Tobin and Tamara had driven in by; but there was no road, no hangar, and no sign of civilization. The ride down was magnificent. First, they skirted alongside hundreds of buffalo who hardly raised their heads long enough to stop grazing, let alone notice the passing party. Next, they followed the rushing creek through a grove of freshly leafed aspen trees.

CHAPTER 20

It was definitely springtime! Even though the scenery was familiar, it was different. There was more snow on the surrounding peaks, and where there used to be roads and small towns, there were none.

The valley seemed to be more alive and fertile. Mother Earth looked all the more at peace.

The chief signaled for the riders to stop, which they did immediately. The party of five sat atop their horses silent and still. The only movement was the horses perking their ears. They had spooked, glazed eyes that were ever alert for the slightest movement of an approaching predator. The horses' only defense was its speed and an instinctive sixth sense, which protected them from danger.

Off to the left was the snap of a branch accompanied by the loud snort of a big animal. The shock of it nearly turned the dark-skinned Indians white as a large bull elk appeared suddenly in front of them. It came out of nowhere. Collectively the party of five let out a large sigh of relief. The elk strolled right in front of them, then as suddenly as it had appeared from the woods, it disappeared back into them. The chief looked to his warriors and their newly acquired guests with bewilderment on his face. Tobin wondered to himself how many times the three of them had witnessed such a thing. He had no idea that they never had. The chief looked to his guests and shrugged his shoulders as they went on their way.

About halfway down the canyon, Tobin noticed a slight shift in the terrain, being that he was familiar with it. It appeared that without the dam that formed Crowley Lake in his time, the flow of the mighty Owens River had cut deep through the valley floor, creating large mesas and deep gorges that followed the river. He inquired to the chief, asking where the village was located. The chief pointed to a place where there was one small island of land that formed a mesa. He could see thirty to forty horses on it, and it made a perfect natural corral about ten miles from where they were. He was shocked that he didn't see any tepees or people, but it could have been the distance or really good camouflage.

Tamara was singing a song of Steve Nicks from Fleetwood Mac, which the chief and his warriors seemed to be enjoying. Tobin was shocked by the change in events but for now was enjoying his new companions. As they drew closer to the corral, Tobin's heart skipped a beat. There standing in the corral, towering over the horses, was his noble companion and friend Camaxtli. Following a close second in height was Tamara's stallion Atlauva.

Tobin rode a notorious breed, the great Percheron. Knights would ride these into battle because of their massive size and strength. The fully armored knight was nothing to this magnificent creature. He whistled to catch Tamara's attention and nodded toward the corral. He knew she saw them because her eyes lit with joy. He made the sign of a zipper over his mouth, and Tamara nodded in recognition. They were now close enough for Tobin to see that six warriors were trying to get a halter on Camaxtli. He was laughing quietly to himself by his steed's noncompliance.

Once the five riders were noticed by the men in the corral, they came running out to greet them. The chief began speaking to the approaching warriors who were skeptically eyeing the two outsiders. Tobin was able to understand much of their conversation. Apparently, his recollection of the language was improving the more he heard it. He related to Tamara what they were saying. They had found their horses three days ago among the buffalo on a hunting trip. It took them the better part of a day to catch them, so they were forced to camp on their way back. They told the chief that they had heard thunder that evening but saw no clouds or lightning.

CHAPTER 21

The chief said that they had heard it as well and went to check the source. That's when they found Tobin and Tamara with their strange furs.

Tamara and Tobin dismounted and started walking toward the corral to check on the condition of their horses. The chief, who was known as Chief Black Wolf, asked Tobin and Tamara if they knew these horses. Tobin started to tell the story of how they were separated when one of the warriors, the chief's son, broke into dispute ownership of the horses. He told Black Wolf that since it was he who had captured the mighty horse, he and he alone had a claim to him no matter how they had been separated. He issued a challenge to Tobin. Tobin understood well what the two were discussing. Tamara asked what the commotion was all about. He explained the developments to her. "Well, it seems that warrior over there wants to challenge me for ownership of Camaxtli. Apparently, a challenge over ownership of horses is a fight that is deemed worthy of a fight to the death. Obviously not a good situation for newcomers to be involved in. So if I do win, that will obviously cause some bad feeling toward us from his friends and family."

"That's crazy," said Tamara. "They're our horses!"

"Yes, but they don't know that, and according to their tradition, the battle is to decide ownership," replied Tobin.

"What are you going to do, Tobin?" she asked.

"I have an idea!" he exclaimed. He looked to Seventh Son and Black Wolf and said, "I have no desire to fight this man. I offer a challenge instead. Whoever can successfully ride the mighty horse, Camaxtli will claim ownership."

The chief knew that name, and it sent chills down his spine to hear Tobin use it! He had heard that in eons gone past the ancients sacrificed their own people to this god, the god of war, fire, fate, and the hunt. Seventh Son, who was issuing the challenge, did not like the idea of this. He told chief Black Wolf that since it was he who had captured the horse and because Tobin would not fight him, the mighty horse belonged to him.

The chief did not see things that way and accepted Tobin's challenge under the condition that the warrior was to go first and Tobin second. It took the warrior and two of his friends almost three hours to halter Camaxtli. Tobin suggested that the warrior take a rest before trying to mount the horse, but his pride would not allow him to do that grave dishonor. He immediately jumped from the corral gate onto the back of Camaxtli. The horse bucked twice hard, but the challenger would not be dismounted. Camaxtli then bolted forward straight to the back of the corral, covering its hundred yards in what seemed like seconds. He mistakenly thought that he had tamed the horse and Camaxtli was his. As quickly as the horse had begun his sprint, he stopped. The rider was not so fortunate as his momentum carried him over the front of the horse and off the cliff that was the corral's natural barrier to his death.

His two friends ran to the cliff's edge to check on their friend's fate while others looked on with solemn expressions. Soon the two warriors wailed out with grief and confirmed what the others were thinking. Tobin looked to the chief and expressed sorrow for the chief's son. The chief was struck with grief and angrily told Tobin to prove his ownership of this mighty horse. Tobin walked into the center of the corral and whistled loudly. Camaxtli perked up his ears and trotted the fifty yards to his owner. When he got to Tobin, he nudged him with his nose as if to make sure he was real and then walked around him one time. He stopped when he was face-to-face with his owner. Camaxtli lowered his head, and Tobin blew a breath into his nostrils while he petted his mane. He then removed the halter. Camaxtli dropped to a knee and Tobin mounted his lifelong friend. He nudged his rear flanks, and Camaxtli took off at a gallop with Tobin holding onto nothing more than his mane.

CHAPTER 22

They made a lap around the corral. Then as they approached the gate that separated the island of land to the mesa, Tobin and Camaxtli straightened their course. All of a sudden, Tobin and his mighty steed jumped from the pen to the mesa, a distance of fifteen to twenty feet. They slowed to a stop, and Tobin dismounted and walked to the face of Camaxtli, who lowered his head to face him. Tobin blew another breath into his nostrils, and the two walked side by side back to the gate.

Tamara looked at Tobin with admiration while the rest looked at him in amazement. The chief waited for Tobin to approach, looked him up and down, and told him that the mighty creature was indeed his spirit horse and a match to be reckoned with.

Tamara ran up to Tobin and threw her arms around him in a warm embrace. She then pulled back and slugged him on his shoulder, saying, "Don't you go around showing off like that. You could have died jumping the gorge like that!"

He answered, "But I didn't. I'm fine, and I didn't have to kill anyone either. My horse did it for me!"

"That's not funny. It's morbid! Besides, it could have been you," she said.

"Wow, you're really starting to sound like my squaw now," Tobin stated.

"Meaning what?" she inquired.

"Meaning I kinda like an ornery woman!" he said.

"Well, you found one!" Tamara replied.

Chief Black Wolf approached them and stated that it is time to see the village now. Tamara and Tobin put their backpacks on and followed Black Wolf. They walked north along the mesa's edge about a quarter of a mile from the corral they started to descend down a trail along the cliff's edge. The trail was porous with a vertical cliff on one side and a thousand-foot drop on the other. Fortunately, after about a hundred yards, it turned into a small subcanyon, making the descent a little less harrowing. Off into the not-too-far distance, they could hear a rushing waterfall. When they rounded a corner, they could see a massive waterfall. It was close to 150 yards wide and fell a thousand feet to the valley floor.

They were now three hundred feet up on the cliff face, and the trail led right into—or more appropriately, behind—the waterfall. It was awe-inspiring! Behind the cascading water was a huge cave at least 120 yards wide and 80 yards high. They were unable to see the end. Throughout the cave were hundreds of tepees. In the front where they could get the most light were various crops. A spring-fed creek zigzagged through the cave that was filled with trout. Children were running about, playing games with puppies chasing behind them. Women were washing clothes in the stream, and groups of men were involved with a variety of tasks. All eyes were on Tamara and Tobin in their brightly colored garments. A group of young ladies were staring and giggling at Tobin as young women tend to do. Tamara was the first to speak and said to Tobin, "I think they like you."

"What's not to like?" he smiled.

"This place is amazing. There must be two hundred families in here!"

Right then Chief Black Wolf explained, "We have 216 families here, 623 people, and 64 dogs. We are totally self-sufficient, safe, and hidden from the Skywalkers."

Tobin asked, "Who are the Skywalkers that you speak of?"

The chief answered, "First we eat, and then I'll explain."

Black Wolf led them to his tepee where his wife ran out to greet him, saying, "What a colorful skin you're wearing, and you brought guests."

Tamara was catching onto the ancient tongue the more she listened. Black Wolf directed his wife to make them lunch, and moments later they were seated around in a circle, enjoying a meal. Black Wolf introduced his wife to his new acquaintances. "This is my wife. Her name is Bright Star." He then went on to inform them that tonight was their spring planting ceremony and that they would be the guests of honor.

Chapter 23

Tamara told Tobin that she needed to freshen up just as he realized that he was smelling pretty ripe himself. He mentioned this to the chief, who said something to Bright Star. She went into the tepee and came back with some garments for the two of them. Then Black Wolf walked them toward the back of the cave where they could see steam rising from a hollow in the rock. He pointed to it, saying, "You can bathe there," and then walked back to his wife. Tamara and Tobin had been speaking as they walked. Most of their conversation centered around how crazy their situation was, how beautiful and impressive the cave was, but most important of all, how they were going to get back to their own time.

As they neared the spring, they passed a young couple that stared at them quizzically, obviously well aware that they were outsiders. There they stood alone staring at what appeared to be a series of seven or eight pools. They appeared to vary in depth and width from three feet to nearly twenty feet across. They felt the water for temperature in the nearest pool, and it was lukewarm. They ventured farther into the cave, testing the pools as they went. The sixth one was not only deep and wide but it was also the perfect temperature.

As they stepped into the pool, the ceiling started to glow like it had suddenly turned into night with the sky ablaze with millions of stars. Tamara splashed Tobin in a playful gesture. Tobin jumped on her shoulders and held her underwater. When he let her up for air, she slugged him on the shoulder, letting him know in no uncertain terms that she was upset. After she gasped for air, she said, "What's wrong with you? You could have drowned me!"

"I was just playing around. I didn't mean to scare you!" he replied.

"You just don't realize your own strength. I'm a woman!" she exclaimed.

"I'm definitely aware that you're a woman and a beautiful one at that!" Then he pulled her closer to him. Staring into her eyes, he said, "According to the locals, you're my squaw, and we have to consummate our marriage."

"Hold it right there, mister! I am not that easy," Tamara said.

He pulled her closer and gave her a long slow kiss that curled her toes, making her ready to ravage him on the spot. He broke free and told her, "That's okay, you're worth the wait."

This time she pulled him in, saying, "Not so fast, ace," as she planted a kiss of her own. They only broke free when they heard the loud giggling of children. One of the children called to them, saying, "I am Coiling Snake, son of Black Wolf. It grows late, and he requests your presence. Tobin and Tamara were surprised to see how dark it had grown. While they were swept away by their passion and the light of the glowworms, time had ceased.

They quickly dressed and made their way to Black Wolf's home. You could feel the excitement in the air. The chief smiled. "Glad to see you fresh and ready to go."

"Yes!" they exclaimed. "This place is remarkable."

The chief was filled with pride at their response.

Black Wolf, Bright Star, Tobin, and Tamara made their way past tepees and couples moving toward the back of the cave. Tobin was astonished at how immense it was as the group crested a ridge and was looking down on a natural amphitheater. There was a large bonfire in the center surrounded by ceremonial dancers dressed in various costumes. The fire sent out cascading shadows that made the dancers appear as giants along the walls and ceiling. One of the warriors noticed the chief and his guests standing atop the amphitheater and let out a loud cry. All action stopped as everyone looked at Black Wolf and began to chant his name. Black Wolf raised his hand to silence the crowd. He then began speaking in the ancient tongue. While his words resonated off of the canyon walls, Tobin translated for Tamara.

CHAPTER 24

"My people, tonight we honor Metzli, the lord of the night, father of the moon, bearer of crops and farming. On this the night of the winter solstice, we give thanks and praise to Metzli for shortening the night and lengthening the days."

His people started to yell and chant. He hushed the crowd once again. "Tonight, an omen has come of age! Just as the God that brought our ancestors to this haven from the Skywalkers had promised, he has returned to vanquish the Skywalkers and lead us out of the underworld to walk again on the fertile lands of our ancestors. Goddess Citalalice, who placed a star to indicate the time of redemption, announces the return of Mextli, who rides mighty Camaxtli."

Tamara was in total astonishment at what was just translated to her and said, "That's us who he's referring to!"

"I suppose it is!" replied Tobin.

Just then the crowd burst with joy at the chief's announcement and dropped to their knees with tears of gratitude along with the chief and his wife. Tobin and Tamara were dazed by the turn of events and stared at each other in astonishment. "What do we do?" asked Tamara.

"I guess we explore the story of this omen," Tobin replied. They both turned and looked to the crowd in bewilderment. When Tobin raised his hands to quiet the chanting, they only got louder.

Finally, the chief rose to quiet the crowd saying, "We have waited long for this day of recompense. Let us sing with joy and praise. Let the Skywalkers be vanquished so we may walk our lands again without the fear of abduction! Let the omen be fulfilled. Now is our time of reckoning."

Tobin looked at the chief and tried to explain that he was mistaken. "I am no god, and Tamara is no goddess. We are mortals just as you are."

The chief quieted him saying, "I make no mistake. The omen is clear. It is as it was told. You are the vanquisher, and she is your consort. Together you will break the chain of events. My people will be able to roam the plains again and hunt the mighty buffalo. Tonight you will meet Red Bear, our medicine man. You will go on a vision quest, and you will see the truth that I speak."

Black Wolf led Tamara and Tobin through the crowded amphitheater. The people bowed in reverence as they passed. They made their way deeper into the cave. It became a maze that was cut deep into the sandstone. Tobin noticed that it was getting lighter instead of darker. He thought this to be very strange. As he looked to the cave ceiling, he noticed he could see what appeared to be stars. Then the moon came into view. Tamara said, "Look, you can see the moon!" There was, in fact, an oval-shaped hole in the ceiling approximately twenty-five yards wide and thirty-five yards long.

Tobin said, "Look over there. Do you see the waterfalls?" The moonlight was reflecting off the waterfalls, giving it a bioluminescent appearance. The waterfall fell into an azure blue pool, which was the most brilliant blue color that either had ever seen. There was a stream that ran from the pool for about forty feet then disappeared into the rocks. Off to the left stood a cylinder-shaped rock and on top of it stood a single tepee. There were stairs circularly cut into the cylinder. Tobin could make out the silhouette of a person sitting in a meditative position to the right of the tepee. The three of them ascended the stairs, and Black Wolf announced their presence to Red Bear.

"Aha! Black Wolf, you bring me company. Please come in, sit, and excuse an old man for not standing to greet you, for I have seen many winters pass," stated Red Bear.

CHAPTER 25

The party stepped into the light of the fire. Red Bear lowered his head to the ground and extended his arms and hands forward, exclaiming, "My god, Mextli it is you! You have long last returned." He looked up to Tobin with tears of joy in his eyes.

Tobin looked to the old man in bewilderment. It was clear to see that Red Bear had indeed seen many winters. To Tobin, he appeared to be in his nineties; but in fact, he was 118 years. His face had been weathered by the sun with wrinkles, and his earlobes hung low from the weight of his large earrings. His nose was large and flat as if he had run into a wall as a child, but his eyes were warm and welcoming, framed as if they were filled with knowledge and wisdom. He rose and hugged Tobin.

"It has been many, many years since our last encounter. I was yet a child and had not received my tribal name. They called me Nokie then. How is it, lord, that you are younger and smaller than I remember? It must be my youth playing tricks on my mind," stated Red Bear. "For sure as the moon is full, you are Mextli in the flesh! Who is this that accompanies you, my lord?"

"Citalalice, for the star has come to the western sky. Your omen has come of age, Red Bear!" said Black Wolf.

"The star, it has come?" Red Bear asked.

"Yes, and the seventh son has fallen, and Camaxtli the mighty horse he rides is here," replied Black Wolf.

Tobin broke into their conversation, stating, "We are not gods. Somehow we have traveled through time!"

Red Bear stopped him this time. "My lord, it is as it was told. You spoke of this nonsense when you last appeared and brought us to this place that has saved your people. You gave me this talisman and told us to seek this material." He presented Tobin with a necklace that had adorned his neck. Tobin's heart skipped a beat.

Tamara could see the shock on his face and said, "What is it, Tobin?"

He told her that the talisman had been his father's and that he hadn't seen it since he was a small child.

"What are you saying? That your father was here?" she asked.

"That's how it appears," he answered.

"That's not possible!" she stated.

"Why not? We're here, aren't we?" Tobin replied. Then he looked at Red Bear and asked, "Have you collected this material?"

"Yes, my lord. Would you like me to show it to you?" Red Bear stated.

"No. Not now. Later after I have had a while to take this all in," he answered.

Tobin and Tamara sat on a log and stared into the fire in silence. Black Wolf and Red Bear joined them, each one lost in their own thoughts. All of a sudden Red Bear and Black Wolf jumped up, fetched two large vases filled with water, and doused the fire! They told Tobin and Tamara to follow them as they ducked into the nearby tepee. As they did so, Tobin asked them what was going on, and Black Wolf told him that the Skywalkers were approaching.

Tobin looked up where he could partially see the sky from the center of the tepee. He could make out some of the stars when suddenly the sky was covered in darkness. He rushed to the tent door and pulled it back enough to see the whole ceiling shrouded in darkness. The blackening of the sky lasted for what seemed like half an hour, but in reality, it was only for several minutes before the stars started to slowly reappear as the airship passed above the opening in the ceiling. Collectively they let out a sigh of relief.

Tobin looked to Tamara, saying, "That airship is huge! How is little old me to vanquish that and whoever built it?" he wondered.

"Uh-huh, you and I are to vanquish them. Remember, I'm your consort!" she exclaimed.

CHAPTER 26

"Yes, Tamara. I haven't forgotten about you. It's just a lot to take in and knowing that my father was here makes it all the crazier. I always thought that he had run out on me and my mom!" Tobin reflected.

"It's more than a little crazy! It's absolutely insane. The whole thing, gods and goddesses, strange airships, time travel. I feel as if I'm in a nightmare and can't wake up!" she expounded.

"So do I, Tamara, so do I." He shook his head in wonder.

While Tobin and Tamara were talking, Red Bear and Black Wolf were busy readying their peyote concoction for Tamara and Tobin to drink. They prepared a small fire in the center of the tepee, and the four of them sat, talking around it. Tobin asked how Red Bear had come into possession of his father's medallion.

Red Bear told a story of how he and some other children were playing at the river's edge close to where the waterfall was. One of the older children was holding back a low-lying branch so the other children could make their way between the tree and the river's edge. A ruckus broke out among the children who had already passed, and one of them bumped into Falling Rock, who was holding onto the branch, causing him to lose his grasp of it. It struck Burning Sage in the forehead with such force that she flew backward and unconscious right into the river. Everything seemed to move in slow motion. Even though there were much older boys around, they all froze with fear, but not little Nokie.

"Abandoning all fear for my own life, I jumped in and grabbed Burning Sage. The weight of her along with the swiftly flowing river was quickly sweeping the two of us toward the edge of the waterfall, but I would not let go of her! Fortunately for the both of us, Mextli was meditating at the edge of the falls, and he reached in with his mighty arms and snatched the two of us up just as the waterfall was sweeping us over. He held me, and I held onto Burning Sage as we dangled in the air above the falls.

"He told me that I reminded him of his son and gave me this talisman. He said that it was very valuable with magical powers and to seek out this metal. Later in my life, I married Burning Sage, and we spent many happy seasons together. She moved onto the spirit world six winters past. I long to see her there, but my work here is not complete. Now you are here to save our people and lead me to the spirit realm.

"Here, my lord, you and Citalalice must drink from the cup of things to be and things gone by. You will see the truth in what I speak. Let your eyes be opened and your ears hear, for the omen is at hand."

Tamara asked Tobin what he thought they should do, and he said, "When in Rome, do as the Romans do." With that said, he took a large drink from the cup and handed it to her. Tamara told him that she had never had peyote before, and he told her to just keep a positive mindset and enjoy the ride.

She said to him, "That shouldn't be a problem. I'm rather enjoying the ambiance of this place, and I'm here with you. You make me feel safe!"

That made Tobin smile as he said to her, "There's no one I'd rather be with."

She blushed and smiled back. Then he suggested that they take a walk. The two of them walked hand in hand down the spiral steps toward the azure-blue pool. Tamara asked Tobin what Red Bear was referring to when he saved the girl from going over the falls and Mextli told him that he reminded him of his son.

CHAPTER 27

Tobin then told Tamara the following story about the time that he, his father, and his brother were walking along the lake's edge. "The trail was narrow, and we were rather high above the water on a cliff face. Our father was in the lead telling us a story as we walked. My older brother was second, and I was bringing up the rear. Little did we know that there was a family of billy goats higher up on the rock face. They dislodged a small avalanche of rocks. One of those rocks hit my brother right in the head, knocking him unconscious. He tumbled off the cliff into the lake and started to sink like a bag of bricks. I didn't even think about it. I just jumped off the cliff into the lake. I swam down for what seemed like forever and finally reached my brother's hand. I was about out of breath when I reached him, but I swam up with him in tow. All of a sudden my father's hand swooped down and pulled us up!"

Tamara was so impressed that she exclaimed, "Tobin you're a hero!"

"Oh, I don't know about that. I just did what came naturally to me. Besides, who knows what would have happened if my dad wasn't there. We would've probably drowned."

"But you didn't. You saved your brother, and that makes you a hero," Tamara replied.

Tobin blushed and changed the topic, saying, "Look at the pool. You can see the fish like they're glowing." The fish weren't glowing, but the water contained thousands of bioluminescent organisms that lit up as the fish swam through them.

Tamara said, "Look at this caterpillar. It's glowing as well!" They looked behind them, and the trail was lit up by the plants they had brushed against, having the bioluminescent properties as well. "This place is magical," said Tamara.

"You're magical, Tamara. You glow with beauty, and you're being solid as a rock through all of this," he stated.

She looked at Tobin, grabbing his hand and placing it on her thigh. She asked, "Does this feel like a rock to you?" Her body was warm, soft, and smooth.

He answered, "No. It feels like heaven." His loins were on fire, and he knew if he held her any longer he'd be as hard as a rock.

She broke away from him and started stripping off her clothes, teasing, "Come on, big boy, catch me if you can!"

Tobin clamored at getting his clothes off. Tamara dove into the water. It lit up around her, giving her the appearance of an angel floating through a cloud. Tobin was right on her tail and swooped her up in his arms. She spun around to face him and slowly leaned in giving him a long sensual kiss. He pulled her in tight, giving her a passionate kiss of his own. They slowly entwined their bodies into one making passionate love. Eventually, they brought their passion to a sandy bank of the pool where they made love for hours.

All of a sudden Tamara stopped Tobin, pushing him away and yelling, "Let me get up quick!" She ran behind a boulder and started to puke.

Tobin made what he knew was a smart-ass comment, saying, "I'm not that bad, am I?"

"No, silly. I think it's the peyote. Besides, you're my first."

"Your first?" he asked.

She replied, "Yes, my first. I've been saving my virtue. Is that such a surprise?"

"These days it's a big surprise!" he responded. Then he told her that he had actually puked a few times after trying peyote for the first time himself. They then swam across the pool to where their clothes were and proceeded to get dressed. Tobin had a hard time taking his eyes off of Tamara. He decided that she was the most beautiful woman he had ever seen. It was at that moment he dedicated to himself that he would one day marry this woman. They were both starting to trip now.

Clouds started forming in the sky as the bats started returning to the cave after their nightly feeding, appearing like a cyclone as they funneled through the hole in the cave's ceiling.

CHAPTER 28

The clouds started to streak across the sky, causing shadows to dance throughout the cave as the clouds floated from west to east, covering the moon's glow. They could hear the singing and chanting from the spring festival rising and falling to the rhythm of the drum. The peyote was having its full effect on the vision seekers. While they were hand in hand, they were miles away in thought, each lost in the events that had befallen them and being swept away in the ecstasy of their love for one another. The sound of thunder rolled in the distance as the rain started falling from the sky. Tobin started counting the timing between the sound of the thunder as it echoed off of the cave walls. He could tell that the heart of the storm was fast approaching.

Tamara got up and went to where the water was raining down. She started twirling and dancing with her arms raised to the sky. Tobin loved her innocence and was admiring her playfulness when his heart was filled with horror. Tamara had just been struck by a bolt of lightning! The sound of the strike and the thunder that followed was deafening as it reverberated off the cave walls and ceiling. Tobin could not believe his eyes, for Tamara continued to twirl and dance as if nothing had happened. Tobin was not the only one to witness this because Red Bear and Black Wolf had seen the strike as well. They looked at each other, saying, "Truly she is Citalalice, the goddess, for no mortal could survive such a thing." Tobin ran to Tamara, who was aglow with brightness. When he got to her, he noticed that one streak of hair about three inches wide had turned solid white. She looked at him and said, "There you are, my love," and collapsed into his arms.

Red Bear and Black Wolf were at Tobin's side within minutes as he was checking her vitals and her body for signs of burns. Other than the white streak of hair, she showed no signs of burns, and her vitals were fine. The chief and medicine man asked Tobin if there was anything that they could do to assist. Tobin told them that she was suffering from shock and asked Red Bear if he could use his tepee. Red Bear answered, "My home is yours." Tobin then swept Tamara up in his arms and took her to the tepee while Black Wolf and Red Bear followed. Once inside, Tobin laid her on the bearskin rug, which was red, and then Tobin figured out how Red Bear got his name.

The chief and the medicine man were standing at the entrance when Black Wolf stated that she was bright and would be known to his people as the Bright One. Tobin looked back toward Tamara, and indeed she was aglow. He returned to her and covered her with a blanket, checking her vitals one more time. The two onlookers asked once again if there was anything that they could do to help. Tobin told them no, that she just needed her rest, and it had been a very long day as well. Red Bear and Black Wolf left leaving the two of them to rest.

Tobin curled up next to Tamara, who fit perfectly in his arms as if she was a piece of a puzzle that he didn't know was missing. His mind started drifting to the events that had befallen them. He was no closer to an answer of how to vanquish the abductors or how to get him and Tamara back to their own time. His mind was troubled, and sleep came hard. Once asleep, Tobin dreamed the most vivid dream that he had ever had. He and Tamara were climbing Flat Top when their climb started to shimmer. The two of them were climbing the roof section again, but it was nighttime, and the earth was emitting lights much like the lights of the aurora borealis. They were particularly bright and flowing from the canyon where they had camped all the way to and around the base of Flat Top Rock.

CHAPTER 29

They were climbing by the light of their headlamps. This time Tamara was leading as Tobin belayed when all of a sudden Tamara started to shimmer, her headlamp appearing and disappearing from view. Then out of nowhere, the entire roof groaned and gave way. He saw her falling from the rock. Throwing all caution to the wind, he leaped from the rock, catching her in midflight. To his shock, they started to fly instead of falling. The difference was that now he could see city lights all through the valley along with cars on the highways also helicopters and airplanes flying in the sky. As they continued to rise everything moved in slow motion, he heard a loud crash as the roof that had given way struck the valley floor.

All at once, everything went black with the helicopters and airplanes falling from the sky. It came as a flash to Tobin that the valley they had camped in was on the San Andreas fault line, part of the earth's fault lines that harness the earth's magnetic energy. When the kinetic energy from the large roof struck the valley floor, it released a large portion of the earth's magnetic energy, causing an EMP (electromagnetic pulse), thus causing all electronic devices to fail simultaneously. Planes and helicopters went crashing to the ground. The lights of the city went dark, and all but very few automobiles stalled in their tracks.

Tobin awoke to Tamara staring at him. She was, in fact, aglow; and he didn't know if it was from the loss of her virginity or being struck by lightning or both. She said, "Good morning, sleepyhead." It was in fact daylight.

"How long have I been sleeping?" he inquired.

"I don't know. I just woke up myself not too long ago," she answered.

Tobin told her that she had no idea how happy he was to see that she was all right.

"Why wouldn't I be?" she asked.

"What do you remember about last night?" he wondered.

"I remember it was magical. All of it, especially in the pool and on the beach," she said.

"Is that all you remember?" he asked.

"Isn't that enough!" Tamara replied.

"You were struck by lightning!" he implored.

She answered, "Is that what you call it? I call it love!"

"No. Seriously, you were struck by lightning, Tamara!" he emphasized.

"Does that mean you don't love me?" she curiously asked.

"No, Tamara, that's farther from the truth than you can imagine! I've always loved you. Now more than ever! But that aside, you were struck by lightning. Just look at your hair."

"Don't be ridiculous. I'm fine, Tobin."

"Let's go look at your reflection in the pool," he stated.

Tobin and Tamara exited the tepee, finding Black Wolf and Red Bear sitting on a log outside. Red Bear said, "Thank you, Mother Earth and Father Sky. You are well."

Tamara realized that she could understand all that he had said. She replied in the ancient tongue as if it were her first language, "Yes, I feel wonderful. Why?"

Red Bear answered, "You were struck by fire from the sky."

Tamara and Tobin then noticed that the whole village stood surrounding the cylinder rock.

Black Wolf announced to the crowd, "The Bright One has awakened." With that, the crowd bowed in unison and chanted, "Praise to the Bright One!"

Tobin and Tamara descended the stairs and passed through the crowd. No one rose until they had passed. She asked Tobin, "Who is the Bright One?"

"You are, my love. Look into the pool," he told her.

She stared into the pool and contemplated her reflection. She was, in fact, glowing and noticed a streak of hair as white as snow that highlighted her face. She looked at Tobin and said, "Now, that's just weird! I guess I was struck by lightning!"

"I hate to say I told you so," he smiled.

"I don't feel any different. Although, I did have some odd dreams," she stated.

"You do remember taking peyote, don't you?" he asked.

"Yes, vividly, all the way up to dancing in the rain, Then it was as if I was walking through a dream," she replied.

CHAPTER 30

"You passed out shortly after the bolt hit you. I figured you were in shock, so I carried you to Red Bear's tepee and laid you down to rest. I had some pretty lucid dreams myself last night," he shared.

"I know. Your eyes were fluttering like crazy this morning. Do you care to enlighten me?" Tamara asked.

"Tell me yours first," asked Tobin.

"Okay. You and I were walking through the canyon cloaked in blankets of fine gold. There were many people among us. Some were clothed in gold while others carried gold, wood, and logs. At the base of Flat Top Rock, the ones carrying gold split off from the ones carrying the wood and logs. You and I walked to the base of our climb, Shimmer. There was a great flurry of activity going on. Some people were attending to Camaxtli and Atlauva. They were hooking our horses to work harnesses. It appeared as if they were making a large bowl in the earth.

"Atop the rock, they arranged the wood as if they were preparing for a huge bonfire. We started to get geared up to climb, but it was close to dusk, and I wondered why we would be starting so late. Then I woke up curled in your arms, enjoying the heat from your body, and that's that!"

Tobin exclaimed, "That's not that. That's it! You're amazing. I love you!"

She asked, "What are you talking about?"

"I'll explain later, but right now we need to gather some intel," Tobin said. They walked hand in hand back from the pool to Red Bear's tepee where Black Wolf and Red Bear were in conversation.

Tobin looked at Red Bear and, pointing to the talisman around his neck, asked, "You have gathered this material?"

"Yes, my lord, just as you told me to do," Red Bear replied.

Then Tobin looked to Black Wolf and asked him to disperse the people and take them to the gold that they had gathered. Black Wolf answered, "Of course, your wish is my command." So the people were dispersed to go about their business, and he directed Red Bear to rest his old bones. But Red Bear would have none of that. Then Red Bear guided Tobin, Tamara, and Black Wolf deeper into the cave. Tobin was surprised at how agile Red Bear was for a man of his age, but then he really didn't know just how old he was so he asked the chief who was walking next to him. The chief proceeded to tell him and Tamara that Red Bear was 118 years old. They both exclaimed that it was incredible. Black Wolf thought to himself that the gods were crazy because they lived forever, yet they find Red Bear's age incredible while it's their immortality that was truly incredible.

The party of four walked for a good quarter of a mile and had to light torches to guide their way. To their surprise, Tamara was still glowing like a lamp in the dark. Her three cohorts deduced that it was her aura that was casting the light that surrounded her.

As they continued, Tobin and Tamara could see some light coming from a side chute down and to the left. They surmised that it was another entrance into the cave system. As they turned a corner, they could see how wrong they were. The side of the cavern was in fact overflowing with gold in all kinds of form. There were nuggets, bars, cups, plates, jewelry, and even a sword all in different fashions and brilliance.

Tamara asked Tobin, "How could they have made such skilled and complicated pieces of gold?"

"I haven't a clue. Let's ask them." Then he turned to Red Bear and asked the question.

"You taught us the art of metallurgy, my lord. Do you not remember?" Red Bear answered.

Tobin's dad had, in fact, taught him the art of refining gold and casting different shapes and designs. "Yes! Yes, I remember, Red Bear. I was just testing you!" he told him.

CHAPTER 31

Tamara and Tobin were amazed to see how much gold they had amassed. "This is quite impressive," Tobin stated to Red Bear and Black Wolf. They were pleased that Metzli approved. Tobin then explained to them that he needed the gold to be made into thin long strips of six feet width and asked them how long it would take them to produce forty or more that were eighty feet long and six feet wide. He wanted thin strips of gold similar to aluminum foil. They determined it would take them about three weeks or more. Tobin told them to get started on it right away. Tamara wanted to know what he had in mind, but he told her "I'll tell you later. Right now we have work to get done!"

He then began assisting Red Bear and Black Wolf in setting up the kiln. Smelting oar into foil thin widths and lengths required the help of strong young men. Red Bear suggested to Black Wolf that he gather them for the chore at hand and that they bring a load of coal with them. Much fuel was going to be needed for the task ahead of them. After Black Wolf left, Tamara, Tobin, and Red Bear built fire from the existing fuels that lay around the kiln. They did this for heat as well as light. Tamara and Tobin couldn't help the feeling of unease that overcame them being surrounded by darkness. It sent chills down their spines, but Red Bear didn't seem to notice or even care about the black that engulfed the fringes of where they were.

The three of them were sitting around the fire when Tamara asked Tobin to explain his plan. Tobin began by saying, "Last night, after our dip in the pool"—he looked at Tamara and winked—"you started dancing in the rain and got struck by lightning although you didn't go down at first. It was as if it had no effect on you. Then I ran to you and you collapsed into my arms."

"Yes. I remember all that. You told me about it," interrupted Tamara.

"Red Bear and Black Wolf were at our side in only a couple of moments, and I carried you to the tepee," he continued.

"Thank you, my love," Tamara interjected.

He went on, saying, "The pleasure was all mine, my queen. Anyway, I laid you to rest but had difficulty falling asleep. My mind kept racing back to the elk, the mouse, and the owl. Then with your being struck by lightning, I kept thinking that there must be some sort of connection between them."

Red Bear was listening intently and commented, "An elk, a mouse, and an owl. Very interesting."

Tobin jumped in, asking, "Do you know the meaning?"

Red Bear shook his head no but said, "I don't know the story. It hasn't been finished yet."

Tobin let out a sigh and continued, "Finally I fell asleep and had a spectacular dream. Tamara, you and I were climbing Shimmer by headlamp. You were leading the climb and fell. Something went wrong, and you kept falling, so I unclipped myself from the belay and jumped after you."

Tamara exclaimed, "You're so brave, my hero!"

He went on. "When I caught you, we stopped falling and were flying instead, but somehow we had jumped forward in time! The valley was covered with city lights from one end to the other. You could see airplanes and helicopters. The earth was alive with colors of its own just as you appear now. Then we heard a loud crashing sound, and we turned to see the roof that we had climbed was falling to the ground. As it hit the earth, the automobiles stopped, and the planes and helicopters went crashing to the ground!"

"So what's that got to do with little old us?" she asked.

Tobin explained, "I wasn't sure until you told me your dream, and I put them together. For a few years now, I have been studying the ley lines of the earth and its natural magnetic fields. I'm quite certain that the earth is a giant living organism and speculate that the earth's magnetic fields are her pulse and that the ley lines and fault lines are her vital organs. Too much pressure to one of these lines, and boom, a natural disaster of one sort or another happens."

"Such as what?" asked Tamara.

CHAPTER 32

"Such as an earthquake, a tsunami, a volcanic eruption, or even worse. Say a polar ice cap shifts, causing a tidal wave miles high and the next ice age, or it could be something on a smaller scale but just as devastating such as an electromagnetic pulse or magnetic shifts in the earth's pulse. Either way, it would wipe out the electric grid, causing all electronic devices to fail."

"You're a genius, Shadow Hawk," she said, using Tobin's Indian name. "But how does that help us get home?"

He answered, "I'm not sure, Tamara. I'm not even sure we can generate a large enough electric magnetic pulse to bring down that ship, but then you told me that in your dream, people were clothed in gold and were digging a huge bowl-shaped dish. With gold being so malleable and such a good conductor of electricity, I realized that you were talking about making a howitzer of sorts that could, in fact, direct an electromagnetic pulse."

"I'm glad you know what my dream was about because I didn't have a clue!" she remarked.

"For some reason, I believe you know much more than you lead onto," Tobin surmised. He thought to himself how mysterious the female species was and that they would never cease to amaze and bewilder him.

Tamara asked, "How do we get that roof section to fall when it seemed to be totally solid while we were climbing it?"

He answered, "I'm working on that. I have an idea. It's a long shot, but it's all I've got considering our current situation. I've got one box of ammunition in my pack and five rounds in my pistol. I can make three maybe four pipe bombs out of the small search-and-rescue shovel that I always carry in my pack."

Tamara, perplexed, said, "Hold up a minute. That roof is 120 feet across and 20 feet wide. How will four homemade pipe bombs possibly bring that down?"

He told her, "Look, if we set the detonation to go off simultaneously and get them deep enough to be approximately midway from the base to the apex, it just might work."

Tamara then asked, "How do you propose to get them to that depth? We only have the Bosch drill with two four-inch drill bits and two dead batteries."

Tobin answered her, "I think I can make solar panels out of gold to charge the batteries. I'm still working on a plan for the drill bits."

"Well, if anyone can do it, I believe that you can, Tobin!" she remarked. With that said, they went to work, laying out the game plan to Black Wolf and Red Bear, who had dozed off during their conversation.

For the most part, the chief and the medicine man were understanding. But when they mentioned the location of where they intended to do this, the color fell from both of the men's faces. Tobin and Tamara felt as though a dense fog had filled the air and settled. Black Wolf and Red Bear broke off and were talking among themselves. Tamara asked Tobin if he knew what the change in demeanor was about, and he told her that he had no idea but intended to find out. He looked at both men and asked them what the problem was all about. Red Bear stepped forward and explained, "Lord Metzli, when you last appeared, it was your supreme order that the land you speak of never be entered. It has always been known to our people as having mysterious powers, and you yourself said that it is a place that swallows people.

"Very few of those who have mistakenly entered there ever returned, and those who did return speak nonsense. They speak of people sitting in strange bubbles traveling to and fro on the land and in the air, also of giant monsters that roam the land, eating people and other monsters like themselves. They speak in strange tongues and craziness. It was you who declared it as a sacred land, and we have kept your command."

Tamara looked to Tobin, and he started to explain what was said when she stopped him and told him, "I understood all that was said."

Tobin's shocked expression gave him away. She continued, "What can I say? I'm a fast learner. Follow my lead." She then raised her voice, and it came booming off of the cave walls as she shouted, "Metzli, the great vanquisher, has spoken."

CHAPTER 33

"Do as he has commanded before he transforms to Metzli, the storm god, and swallows you with a raging storm. I, Citalalice, will place any person who vanishes during this quest as a star in the heavens. He or she will be known by their people and be known as an immortal to shine on their people forever. This I promise. I, Citalalice, the Bright One, goddess of the stars, give eternal life to the people!"

To their surprise, the villagers were closer at hand than they expected. At first, they appeared as shadows in the dark. One by one, each group lit a torch, and before they knew what to think the cave was ablaze with hundreds of flickering lights as far as the eye could see. Black Wolf looked to Tobin and Tamara and explained that it was a sign from the villagers that they were in accordance with their wish. Red Bear looked on in bewilderment at the flickering lights.

Tamara looked at Tobin, saying, "It looks like we've got our manpower. Let's get this party rolling!"

At that very moment, an owl flew right over the top of them and disappeared into the cave wall. Tobin's mind flashed to the beginning of their journey, the elk, the mouse, and the owl. Within an hour, the furnaces were roaring with heat, and the smelting process was underway.

The next process would be considerably more complex, for there were provisions to be gathered and logistics put in place. Tamara and Red Bear set out to assemble provisions such as food, water, tepees, and medical supplies while Black Wolf and Tobin went to work on picking men and gathering the horses. Black Wolf told Tobin that they had sixty-five horses in the corral on the mesa, and if they counted Camaxtli and Atlauva, they had sixty-seven. In the corral at the base of the canyon, they had another forty-two horses. He informed Tobin that it would take a day's ride to bring them up to the mesa corral. Tobin asked Black Wolf, "How long will it take us to get to the corral at the base of the canyon?"

The chief looked at him with a smile on his face and said, "About one full step of the sun."

Tobin had no idea what that meant, but assuming it was 1,500 feet to the valley floor, it would be about half a day's hike. He asked the chief to dispatch runners immediately to fetch the horses. Black Wolf looked back to Tobin with disappointment strewn across his face. Tobin couldn't help but notice the change in his demeanor and asked the chief if there was a problem. The chief told him, "No, lord. I was just hoping you, Citalalice, and I would go to fetch the horses."

Tobin responded, "There is much to be done, and our time should be used wisely."

"Yes, my lord. I just thought that you would like to see the completion of the escape routes that you started many moons ago," Black Wolf answered.

That struck a chord with Tobin. He was now quite interested in seeing the work his father had started. Tobin and Black Wolf found Tamara and Red Bear surrounded by a flurry of activity. There were women and children grinding corn along with a variety of other grains. They were also baking both leavened and unleavened bread and smoking an assortment of game. Tobin asked Tamara how it was going, and she told him that they should be ready to go within a day. "That's perfect," exclaimed Tobin. "The chief and I would like you to go with us to retrieve the horses at the base of the canyon."

She replied, "I don't know, Tobin. There's so much yet to be done."

Tobin told her, "It seems to be a pretty big deal to Black Wolf that we see their emergency exit system that my father had helped design and started."

Red Bear overheard their conversation and hurried over to join the two. "Ah yes, Citalalice and Metzli, you must go through our emergency escape route."

"Wait a minute, how did you understand what I just told Citalalice?" Tobin inquired.

CHAPTER 34

"You taught it to my father, my lord, who taught it to me, and I taught it to others," Red Bear replied as he made a sweeping gesture toward his people.

Tamara looked at Tobin in surprise as he said to Red Bear, "You mean you understand everything we've said?"

He answered plainly, "Yes, my lord."

Tamara whispered to Tobin, "I hope we didn't say anything inappropriate."

Tobin whispered back, "I'm pretty sure we're okay. Let's go see what this escape route is all about."

Tamara and Tobin went to Black Wolf, telling him that they needed to get their packs before going to get the ponies. Black Wolf explained that they wouldn't be needing to get any gear because everything that they need is at the base of the canyon.

"But we will be traveling in the dark," said Tobin. "It will be dusk in less than two hours, and it'll take longer than that to reach the base of the canyon!"

Black Wolf said, "Oh no, my lord, much less time than you perceive."

Tamara gave Tobin an inquisitive look. He could only shrug his shoulders, and they followed Black Wolf toward the entrance to the cave. As they passed the pool where they had made love, Tamara and Tobin shared a smile between themselves. It was daylight now with the sun shining brightly through the hole in the cave ceiling. The crystal clear pool had all the colors of the rainbow emanating from the darker colors in the center to the lighter ones around its edge. Many of the trees and shrubs that they couldn't see at night were now visible and abundant. They were filled with birds, butterflies, and flowers, as a lizard darted across the rock. Tobin and Tamara now realized just how magical and alive the cave really was. Instead of passing the cylinder rock that was Red Bear's abode, they bore left going past the creek that filtered from the pool. Black Wolf led them to an offshoot cavern that broke to the right.

The light from the vulva-shaped gap in the ceiling had dimmed considerably, but there was light at the end of the tunnel, and it brightened as they walked on. They could now hear the sound of rushing water and Tobin noticed four teardrop-shaped holes cut into the rock. There was a cascading waterfall coming from above that formed a shallow pool before it continued its descent to the valley floor. Black Wolf led them to the teardrop holes where water was flowing into them at a steady pace. He then pointed to the holes, exclaiming that this was their escape route.

"Which one should we take?" asked Tobin.

Then Black Wolf told them that they all led to the same place and that they should each take one at the same time. He then proceeded to tell them to keep their arms crossed over their chest, saying, "We will go on three. One! Two! Three!"

They went in feet first with the current of the water gradually pulling them forward. It was a dark tunnel, really dark, and in an instant, they were screaming as they went downward at an incredible pace. They must have fallen two hundred feet or more. It was hard to tell in the dark. Slowly the grade and speed of their descent mellowed but not by much. Every once in a while, there were streaks of light as they turned to the left and then back to the right and vice versa as the steepness varied as well. They were still traveling at a fast pace with water splashing everywhere. Tobin could hear Tamara screaming, but they weren't out of fear. They were screams of excitement mixed with laughter. He could also make out the sounds of laughter coming from Black Wolf. Then the darkness ended, and he could see Black Wolf shooting down a natural rock side off to his right and Tamara off to his left and slightly behind him.

They were traveling through narrow individual canyons with the colors of the rocks being a beautiful hew of burnt red mixed with streaks of black and beige. Occasionally the bottom would drop out, causing his stomach to get caught up in his throat as he picked up speed.

CHAPTER 35

It was amazing how much distance they had covered in such a short time. Tobin's partners would come into view only to disappear behind another fin of the canyon. Tobin heard Black Wolf let out a scream and then a big splash. He soon found out why as he was flying through the air falling what felt like fifty feet but, in reality, was only twenty feet into the brightest bluish-green pool that he had ever seen. He then heard Tamara scream as she got spat out of the rock only four feet away. She came up out of the pool, saying, "Let's do this again!"

Tobin now understood Black Wolf's desire to fetch the horses and thought to himself that this was the idea where waterparks must have come from. The three of them spent some time swimming in the pool at the base of the canyon. "This is good for the soul," Tobin thought, "to take a break from the immediate dilemma and smell the roses so to speak."

The base of the canyon was 150 yards wide and ran about five miles in either direction. The rock cliffs that shrouded it were 1,500 to 1,800 vertical feet on both sides. Black Wolf told his companions that going north would lead to the head of the canyon where three rivers merged into one. Going south would lead to the valley basin. Going either direction was tricky, and only the ones who knew the river and where to forge it could successfully navigate their way out. Tobin asked which route they'd be taking, and Black Wolf looked to the cliff pointing toward the west. Tamara and Tobin looked at each other wearily. Tobin said to her, "I shouldn't have asked." It looked to be an impossible feat as he noticed a zigzagging pattern that appeared to be painted on the side of the cliff. He secretly said to himself, "I hope that's not it." But he knew that it was.

There were pueblos carved into the rock cliffs on both sides. It took a little time for the villagers to realize who was in their presence, but once Black Wolf announced his guests, every one of them bowed in reverence. This made Tamara and Tobin very uneasy and pressured to free them from their lot. Tamara thought to herself how pristine the valley was and wondered why people think the grass always looks greener on the other side.

Black Wolf suggested that they get some rest before they set out on their drive and motioned toward one of the pueblos. The pueblos were small containing two small rooms that Tobin assumed were bedrooms and a room with a table and three chairs. There were some shelves cut into the back wall holding pottery of various shapes and sizes. A short stout Indian woman guided them to the table and instructed them to sit while she prepared some food for them. Black Wolf tried to tell the older woman that they just wanted to take a much-needed rest when she slapped him on the backside of his head, telling him, "That is no way to speak to your mother in front of guests." Black Wolf shrugged his shoulders and introduced his mother, whose name was Moon Song. Moon Song looked at Tobin and said, "You are much smaller than I remember, but that was many moons ago. My mind must play tricks on me in my old age."

"You're not the first person to tell me that," replied Tobin.

Tobin, Tamara, and Black Wolf sat at the table while Moon Song wasted no time doting over them, first by serving tea, then a salad with nuts and fresh fruit, followed by the most amazing buffalo steaks Tobin and Tamara could remember. After their meal, Moon Song guided them to their rooms. The rooms were aglow from lamps fueled by animal fat, and the smell was enchanting. The walls of the rooms were painted with designs of people in pursuit of their game, animals in a field, and a rather peculiar one of an airship with people fleeing from it being chased by four armed monsters. The sight made Tobin grimace, reminding him of his appointed task that he had taken on, dragging Tamara into it without even asking.

CHAPTER 36

Moon Song brought furs for bedding and instructed them to take some rest, indicating that she would wake them when it was safe for their journey. "How is it that your mother knows when it's safe to travel?" Tobin asked Black Wolf.

"She is a seer of visions, though they're not always correct. Now get some rest, my lord. I will see you when the time is right," Black Wolf replied as he exited the room.

A light breeze meanders through the pueblo making the figures of man and beast come alive, dancing in the firelight of the flickering lantern. Off in the distance, he could hear the rushing water of the river as it ate its way through the rock and sediment, impeding its journey to the ocean. Tamara broke the silence by saying, "That was really fun today! And to think your father started those escape tunnels. It must have been quite the undertaking."

"Yeah. It is pretty cool to know he didn't run out on my mother and me," Tobin answered as he went to Tamara and lay down next to her. Her body was radiating heat, and he drew near to her. Her eyes were a radiant hazel, the firelight causing them to sparkle as if fireworks were going off in her eyes. Her silky black hair was shiny and smooth as it lay spread out around her shoulders, breast, and head like rays projecting from the sun. Her skin was soft as cotton and a honey-bronze color. She was beauty personified, and Tobin was falling in love with her.

They made love for hours and lay crumpled together as one flesh as they drifted off to sleep. It was still two hours before dusk when Moon Song woke them from their slumber. The air was cold, causing Tamara to draw farther into her covers. Black Wolf beckoned them to join him at the table, persuading them with hot cups of tea. Reluctantly they donned their clothing and joined him as Moon Glow quickly provided the three with a breakfast consisting of scrambled eggs, fresh bread, and porridge. They ate in relative silence, which was only broken by the howl of a lone coyote.

Black Wolf rose to his feet, stating that the horses were ready. Moon Glow brought them jackets for their ride and bid them farewell and safe travels. The air inside the pueblo was cold, but upon stepping outside, they were greeted by what felt like a frost wall. They could see their breaths, which appeared as if they were sending out individual smoke signals. They descended to the riverbed where two young men and twenty-eight horses awaited them. Four of the horses had already been saddled and waiting for their mounts. Tamara chose first, picking a beautiful paint spotted with patches of black and dark brown. Tobin chose a sorrel-colored horse of about a ten-hand height. Black Wolf and one of the two men mounted the two remaining horses. Black Wolf took the lead toward the direction of the zigzags that Tobin had noticed the day before.

The canyon cliff was sheer, dark, and ominous. The closer they got, the more ominous it appeared, and before they knew it they were at its base, staring upward. Tobin was the first to break the silence by stating, "That's a long way up!"

"That's putting it mildly," Tamara said.

Black Wolf had guided them to the base of the trailhead. The young man who accompanied them dismounted and began untethering the horses as Black Wolf took the lead position followed by Tamara in second and Tobin third.

Tamara asked, "Why is he untying the horses?"

"So if one falls, he doesn't drag the rest of us with it!" Tobin replied.

"Oh! That's a good reason," she agreed.

After the brave untied the last pony, he rolled his rope, mounted his steed, and took up a position at the rear of the line. It was still dark as they started their ascent of the cliff. They could see the breaths of the horses hanging heavily in the air as well as their own amid the cold air. It was still an hour or more before sunrise.

CHAPTER 37

Tobin shuddered from the cold and tried to draw his extremities closer to his body for warmth. He could see Tamara trying to do the same and appreciated the fact that she didn't complain as most women he knew would be doing by now. No, not Tamara, she's different from other women not just in toughness. She was brave as well and carried herself with a sense of nobility not in the pompous sense but more in a virtuous sense. Yes, that was it. "Virtue, beauty, and bravery," Tobin thought; and he knew he was falling for her hard.

They had been climbing for a good fifteen minutes. The valley now lay far below. The trail was narrow, but the rock was solid and the horse knew enough about preserving their lives. That one slip would end it; therefore, the hoof placement was slow and steady. As they gained in height, they also became more exposed on the cliff now at 500 feet with another 1,100 to 1,200 to go. Tobin secretly wished he was tied in with his climbing gear with Tamara on belay. She was secretly wishing the same thing. She had to raise her leg to prevent it from being smashed between the horse and the sandstone. Tamara could see the sun starting to shine on the cliff high above them, and she longed to bask in its warmth.

They slowly and methodically made their way up the cliff, all of them silent, lost in their private thoughts, with the only sound being the clopping of the horses' hooves as they steadily rose. The riverbed was now far below them when Black Wolf pointed to a particular boulder telling them that they were at the halfway point.

Sitting atop the horses, Tamara and Tobin felt uneasy. It's not natural to give control of your movement over to another human, let alone a horse. Yet here they were, a thousand feet above the valley floor, with their lives resting in a horse that neither of them was familiar with. Tobin couldn't decide if it was an act of bravery or stupidity. He figured probably the latter and kept riding. High above them, they heard the cry of a hawk, and looking in that direction Tobin could see that they were getting closer to the sunshine and that meant warmth. His fingers, toes, and ears were frozen; and his nose hurt from breathing in the cold air. He knew the others were suffering the same fate.

What he didn't notice was that the hawk had dropped a small snake from its talons just before it screeched. Black Wolf and Tamara had just turned a corner when Tobin heard the rattler. Black Wolf's horse reared and went backward into Tamara's horse. There was nowhere for her horse to go with Black Wolf in front and Tobin behind. Its forward hooves were forced off the trail, and before Tamara knew what was happening, she was flying through the air. Throwing her arms up in desperation, she was amazed to grab hold of something. That something was Tobin's arm as he reached out to grab her, nearly getting dragged down with her. Tamara's horse clipped another horse farther down the cliff, sealing its fate along with the one she had been riding. Black Wolf regained control of his ride. Reaching behind himself, he produced a blade and flung it at the small rattler, dislodging its head from its body. Tobin swung Tamara back onto the trail. Her heart surged with adrenaline, making it hard for her to catch her breath. Tears welled up in her eyes, more for her horse than for herself, but she forced them back.

The brave bringing up the rear of their line yelled up to them to check their status. It took a moment for him to get a reply. "Oh my god! That was terrifying," stated Tamara.

Tobin and Black Wolf were quick to agree. Tobin offered Tamara an arm to get up on his horse, but she quickly declined, saying she'd rather walk for a bit. Neither Tobin nor Black Wolf could blame her.

CHAPTER 38

Black Wolf said that they should get moving as the horses were getting restless. Tamara moved up to take the lead, and they started again, but it wasn't long before she was winded. She picked out another horse and rode bareback the rest of the way with no further incidents.

Upon reaching the top, they all dismounted to stretch their legs and retether the horses. It was a brilliant morning. The sky was lined with stratus clouds, which gave the appearance of a large sapphire wave rolling over the high desert. The temperature was steadily rising, warming numb toes, fingers, and noses, easing the tension in their sore, tight muscles. The four riders gathered in a circle holding hands they prayed to the Sky Father and the Earth Mother for the loss of their horse and safety for the remainder of their trip. Black Wolf chanted, "May Tielia's, the horse's spirit, run the sky forevermore and guide us in our venture to free our people forever."

They mounted their horses and rode onward to the corral without any more problems. Upon arriving there, they were met by a flurry of activity. Supplies and rations were being brought from the cave to the corral in well-fashioned saddle packs. Red Bear had definitely been studious in his efforts. Tobin was relieved to be off the horse. Truth was that he and Tamara had become so in sync with Atlauva and Camaxtli that they felt uneasy on any other mount. Informed that Red Bear waited for them in the cavern, they took a short rest to eat and refresh themselves before heading that way. Tobin was eager to get working on the solar batteries for the Bosch drill, for without them their plan would be thwarted.

Upon arriving at the cave, they were greeted by Red Bear and sixty of his braves. He informed them that the lengths of the gold foil had been fashioned and that the party would be ready to travel by first light. The fact was that Tamara and Tobin needed a break from activities. They broke away from the group and went to the mineral hot springs where they were enjoying some alone time and discussing the events that had befallen them. Tamara was the first to chime in. "Mr. Shadow Hawk, I must admit that when the tribal council elected me to accompany you into our sacred lands, I expected an adventure. So far this has dramatically exceeded my expectations. Never in a million years did I expect anything remotely like this. Do you have any idea on how to get us back to our own time?"

"To tell you the truth, Tamara, I haven't stopped thinking about it since the event. As I told you earlier, I've been studying the earth's ley lines and its electromagnetic field. It just so happens that Flat Top Rock happens to be right on top of one of the top three places that are the earth's strongest. From what I know of physics which, I mind you, isn't a lot, the gravitational pull accompanied with electromagnetic energy can stretch and swallow time. In theory that is" he answered.

"Well, that's all fine and dandy, but how do we reverse it?" she asked.

"I don't know. But when the sun comes out tomorrow, I think I might. At any rate, I'm still working on it. For now, though, we've got another project," Tobin said.

"And what, pray tell, is that?" she asked.

"We have to gather some bat guano before we leave," he replied.

"You must have a mouse in your pocket because I could swear that I heard *we*," she said.

"Oh come on. You can't be afraid of a little shit, are you?" he inquired.

"It's not so much the shit as the shitter. What do you need it for anyway?" she asked.

"I'm planning on using it as an accelerant for the fuse and possibly a little extra bang for the pipe bombs, supposing I can find some saltpeter, potassium nitrate, charcoal, and sulfur," he explained.

"That's all fine and dandy, but I think I'll pass on the guano gathering," she replied.

"Oh come on now, you're telling me that after all we've gone through, you're scared of bats?" he asked.

"Terrified!" Tamara exclaimed.

"All right then, let's find Red Bear. I'll handle the shit detail, and you can get some rest," Tobin said.

CHAPTER 39

"I've been thinking that you mentioned the need to lengthen our drill bit, and I've got an idea," said Tamara. "I figure we could melt down some of our friends and our climbing gear and use them for extending the rods for the drill bits. We just need to flatten the drill end of the bits and make a mold for the cast iron out of rock."

"You know what, Tamara?" he said.

"What Tobin?" she asked.

"I love you more every day. That's an awesome idea. We will need some kind of bit for bearing the holes wider for the pipe bombs also," he answered.

"Gee, Tobin, being a little needy aren't we. Do I have to come up with everything around here?" Tamara teased.

"Haha, Tamara, just be happy you got out of the shit detail," he jokingly replied.

"That's goddess Citalalice to you, mere mortal!" she smiled.

"Woman, I knew it would go to your head," he joked.

"Sorry, Lord Mextli, should I bow and curtsy to you?" she said.

Tobin laughed, kissed her, and then waved her off. "I'll see you in a few hours," he said as he trotted off to find Red Bear.

Tamara finished dressing and went off to find Black Wolf. She found him in the village sitting with a young man. She could easily tell from the looks of the child that he was Black Wolf's son. It suddenly dawned on her that other than his mother, neither she nor Tobin knew anything of the chief's family. Tamara decided to inquire.

Black Wolf had gone onto explain his wife and two sons, other than the one present, had been kidnapped by the Skywalkers—they and many others, including Red Bear's wife, son, and daughter, all at different times, making his agony all the more relentless.

Tamara's heart bled for all of them. She could see the anguish in Black Wolf's eyes. She knew right then that she and Tobin must succeed. She made a personal vow of it. Inspired by a new sense of zeal, she told Black Wolf of her needs. The three of them then made their way back to Red Bear's to retrieve the climbing gear and from there to the kilns to make the mold.

Meanwhile, Tobin was being guided by a couple of Red Bear's braves deeper into the cave where the bats nested. Tobin could tell by the pungent odor that they were getting closer. Although he would never admit it to Tamara, he was glad that it was evening so the bats would be out feeding.

Back at Red Bear's camp, Tamara was looking to the opening in the cave ceiling and thought she was seeing a twister coming down through the cave, but instead she quickly realized that it was bats—literally thousands of them—almost completely blocking out the sky. She asked Black Wolf why it looked like a tornado, and he explained that the bats always turned to the left when exiting a cave, and with that many exiting at once, it did indeed appear like a tornado. When they arrived at the kilns, Tamara drew a template of the bit extensions that she desired into the sand. The metalsmith assumed she wanted them to be made out of gold and turned to start fashioning the mold, but she drew him back and handed him one of the clamping devices. He began working the device in his hand, amazed at the mechanics of it. Tamara went on to explain that gold would be too malleable, making it unusable for their purpose. She instructed him to melt the cams to fabricate the extensions. He was reluctant to destroy such an amazing device, but being that she was the goddess Citalalice, he complied with her wishes. He was delighted to help after she promised to show him the purpose of the remaining cams at a later time.

Tobin was happy to find the guano in the right stage of decomposition. Even more pleasing was that he and the braves were able to grab what they needed, exiting that part of the canyon before the bats returned. It was bad enough that they had to deal with the stench, but the entire floor moved like ripples in a pond from all the insects that fed on it. It was only after a full thirty-minute washing under the waterfall and a good swim in the pool that the feeling of bugs crawling on him subsided.

CHAPTER 40

He was grateful that Tamara hadn't joined him. He never wished to go through that revolting experience again, let alone drag her through such a nasty ordeal.

They both met up at Red Bear's camp for a late meal and to discuss the logistics of the events to come. Black Wolf's mother, Moon Song, had indicated that they should be free to travel between now and the coming new moon but needed to use extreme caution while working in the sacred lands and during nighttime. This was not new news to Red Bear, who told them that they would travel by day and set up camp just below the sacred lands. From the description of the land, Tobin figured that it was where the gate had been where they parked the truck and near to the place where they had the run-in with the wolf pack. It would be a full day's ride to the base camp, especially considering the size of their posse.

Red Bear woke Tamara and Tobin an hour before dawn. They drank some warm tea, donned their gear, met with Black Wolf, and headed to the stables. They arrived just as the sun started to crest the horizon and were greeted by nearly a hundred warriors mounted and ready to go chanting Mextli and Citalalice. The atmosphere was electric, and the four newcomers were enamored by the excitement. Black Wolf and Red Bear mounted their horses, followed by Tamara and Tobin, who took time to speak to Camaxtli and Atlauva before mounting them. Atlauva stood a full two hands taller than the native American mustangs while Camaxtli was closer to four hands their senior. Red Bear and Black Wolf led out followed by Tobin and Tamara. The braves bowed their heads in reverence as they road past and led their way out.

Tobin had been on trail rides with friends before, but it was nothing compared to riding with nearly another ninety some riders. The line must have stretched close to a half mile in length. He had no idea how Moon Song knew of the relative safety of the travelers from the Skywalkers. He just prayed her vision was correct, especially considering the length of the expedition and their exposure on the open plains of the valley floor where both trees and cover were sparse. After about four hours of steady riding, they came to the same trail-head that Black Wolf and his braves had led them down. From far off the party must have looked like a large snake making its way up the mountain with sections of it disappearing into the trees as other sections rose out of them at varying heights and intervals. Two hours after entering the trail at the base of the mountain, they reached the first meadow where the mysterious airstrip and hangar used to be or would be eventually, depending on how you looked at it.

Four hours passed till they cleared a small hill and nearing the base of Flat Top Rock. Red Bear and Black Wolf indicated that this is where they would set up base camp and from there work their mission. There was a cliff face that ran about a mile long and 120 feet tall. It made up nearly three-fourths of the entire length of the hill they had just ascended and descended. The cliff side of the hill faced northwest and had a small creek at its base that ran the entire length and down into the valley. There were sections in the cliff that were recessed creating long thin caves. The braves dismounted and started erecting camp in these shelters. Tamara and Tobin went to Red Bear and Black Wolf expressing the desire to erect a base camp closer to the worksite. Red Bear explained that camping any higher was where the craziness occurs and that neither he nor the braves would spend a night any closer than where they were. After what had happened to Tamara and Tobin with the horse in the upper valley, they could understand his reasoning very well. Besides, Tobin was no longer sure if these disturbances were natural phenomena or products of the mysterious Skywalkers.

CHAPTER 41

The camp was erected within an hour. Parties were broken into various groups in different stages of cooking and warming themselves by the fire. Others were grooming and graining their horses. Dusk was quickly approaching as Flat Top Rock, which didn't represent a table at all, loomed in the distance. Tamara looked to Tobin and asked, "What in the world could have cleaved that massive granite spire to level it as it was back in our time?"

"I don't know. I'm not exactly sure when in time we are. It could have been a glacier, a meteor, an earthquake. Who knows. I never imagined it looking as it appears now, that's for sure!" he answered.

They walked for a while in silence, simply enjoying each other's company. Tobin saw some movement on a nearby rise and assumed it was one of the sentries sent out by Black Wolf to keep watch for intruders. He suggested that they make their way back to camp. He desired to gain as much insight into the Skywalkers that Red Bear and Black Wolf could give him. When he and Tamara returned to camp, Red Bear was busy extinguishing the campfire. He told Tamara that Black Wolf was off checking on the other braves, making sure all were accounted for and that sentries were dispatched in proper locations. Also that all fires were extinguished before it was dark. After Red Bear had completely extinguished the fire, he, Tobin, and Tamara retired to a private spot in the cavern where they could talk.

Red Bear began by stating that the Skywalkers started to appear nearly thirty years ago when he was still a young man. At first, they would just see an occasional airship fly over mostly in the evenings when the moon was full or close to it. Once in a while, the ships would appear in day hours but only if the moon was full or mostly full and visible during the day. These initial sightings were common and without occurrence. Then as people got accustomed to their sightings groups would gather in wonder to witness them. That's when the people would suddenly start to shimmer like a mirage, like water in the desert, and whole groups of them would simply vanish. As news traveled through the different tribes, the people became aware of what was happening and no longer gathered to see them. Instead, they would hide in fear.

This was when the Skywalkers first started to appear. They would move as if floating through the air, and once they reached the ground they would scatter, surrounding the people and scaring them out of hiding. They would use their numbers to force the people into groups whereupon they vanished with the Skywalkers. Some of the braves gathered to fight their abductors, but the Skywalkers were giants nine to twelve feet tall with four arms and bulging muscles. Their heads were elongated with broad features. They had forklike tongues and fangs protruding from their mouths. They had the horn of ram atop their heads. Their skin was leathery and grayish white. Some were protected by scales. The people shot arrows at them, and they went right through them. Their roar was deafening. Knives, arrows, and flame did not affect them. They were ferocious and unkillable!

Black Wolf returned from his rounds stating that all was secure and suggested that they all get some rest. Tamara and Tobin snuggled together under the buffalo skin blanket. Tamara was telling Tobin how horrific these Skywalkers must be when something poked her in her thigh. "I'm telling you how scary these things sound to me, and you get horny!" she exclaimed.

Tobin replied, "What can I say? It sounds exciting! Besides you have this effect on me."

"How will I be able to be seen in public with you and, um, your bulge?" she asked.

"I'm hoping we won't have to. I'm a selfish lover. I want you for my own," he replied.

CHAPTER 42

They made love with Tobin holding his hand gently over her mouth, muting her moans of pleasure. Their passion lasting for hours before collapsing on each other as one flesh.

Red Bear woke them at dawn with a warm drink and a hot meal. Then Red Bear, Black Wolf, Tamara, and Tobin gave thanks to the father sky and the earth mother, asking for good fortune and success in vanquishing the Skywalkers.

It took a little over an hour to reach the base of the rock and the valley was still in shadow. The party had split into two separate units. Red Bear, Tobin, and Tamara leading the larger party to the rock for the excavating part of the mission while Black Wolf led the remaining braves to build wood stretchers for the horses to haul timber for a massive fire that they intended to use as a beacon on top of the rock. Since the tree line stopped at roughly ten-thousand-feet elevation, they would need to gather the wood there then transport it around Flat Top Rock to its lower sloping angle.

They would use the horses to haul it as high as possible then use manual labor to get it the remaining four hundred to five hundred feet—a daunting, time-consuming task. It was thought that a massive fire on top of the rock would draw in the Skywalkers hopefully in their airship. That would get it in the approximate location of the EMP they intended to create.

Upon arriving at the base, Tobin set up his solar battery charge where he figured the sun would shine first. He then proceeded to draw a massive oval shaped circle in the dirt and sand at the base of the rock. He did this by his closest estimation of where the massive roof would most likely impact the earth due to its projected fall line. There were several rocks and boulders, some the size of cars, that needed to be dealt with before all-out excavation could occur. Red Bear instructed some of the braves to cut and retrieve some large lumber for rollers and levers to engage in moving the largest of the boulders. Meanwhile, others in the party were busily rolling the smaller rocks out of the circle. Tamara and Tobin busied themselves with constructing a slide and harness for Camaxtli to use his massive power and strength. This would be vital in the moving of the largest boulders. After a group lunch, which consisted of a lot of joking, laughing, and mutual camaraderie—the sight of which instilled in Tamara and Tobin a great deal of comfort—seeing these people working in unity and service to each other was something that they seldom witnessed during their modern time.

After eating lunch, Tamara and Tobin went to check on his custom-made battery charger. He was excited to see that it had worked, and immediately he put the other battery on to receive a charge as well. Next, he needed to check the longevity of the charge. He put a bit into the drill then thought better of it. He didn't want to burn up one of his only two bits so he exchanged it for a branch nearly five-eighths of an inch in diameter with a good fan of foliage on the opposite end. This was done to create friction. He then pulled the trigger, causing the branch to spin in rotation. Red Bear saw this from a distance, dropped what he was doing, and came over to inquire about this amazing device. Tobin explained what it was and how he could drill into rock with it. This device amazed him although he could not discern how wood could cut through stone. Tobin and Tamara smiled at each other. Rather than explain further, they figured some things were better left as a mystery and enjoyed watching Red Bear with a childlike expression on his face.

The rest of the expedition had returned with the wood they needed for the levers and rollers. Tobin left Red Bear to play with his new toy and went to assist with the placement of the materials. After things were in place, he went to retrieve Camaxtli, but on his way, he ran into Red Bear. The drill was still running strong, and he was trying to drill rock with the tree branch, which was now devoid of foliage.

CHAPTER 43

The branch was nothing more than a nub. Tamara had been supervising him to make sure he didn't damage the drill. She stood by with an undeniable smile on her face. Tobin looked at Tamara and said, "It looks like the batteries are holding a full charge!"

Red Bear stopped and told them, "It not work on rock too well."

Tobin and Tamara both smiled.

Red Bear told them that they needed to gather the braves and return to camp.

There were still three hours of daylight remaining, and two of the large boulders had yet to be moved. Tobin reluctantly agreed only after some coaxing by Tamara alluding to a repeat of last night's sexual escapade. Tamara and Tobin headed out as Red Bear gathered the remainder of the party and followed. They picked their way down the game trail that they had ridden in on. It was a bit wider on their way down and would only widen daily as the riders and their horses trod the ground. They reached the point in the trail where the party had split into separate groups. Tobin was not surprised to see Black Wolf and his braves when he turned to look up that trail. He was a little impressed and daunted to see how much wider the trail had grown since they split ways. Tamara and Tobin waved their party past and waited for Black Wolf to catch up with them.

Black Wolf was pleased to see his lords and friends. The three sat talking atop their horses as they let the braves pass and waited for Red Bear, who brought up the rear of the first party. They exchanged pleasantries and briefly discussed the progress on both sides. Pleased by their overall progress, they returned to camp, ate dinner, and took refuge for a good night's rest.

The next day, the work moved quickly since the materials and tools had been fashioned and put into place. Tobin's horse Camaxtli was invaluable in the removal of the large boulders from the excavation site. Once this process was completed, Tobin brushed down his horse and let him graze with his legs hobbled in a pasture close to the worksite. Then he and Tamara left Red Bear and his workers to clear and smooth out the remaining rock and rubble from the long oval crater they had fashioned.

Tobin mounted a fresh horse while Tamara rode on her stallion Atlauva past many of the hard-working braves. They all bowed in reverence as they rode by. They were still having difficulty in knowing how to react to being held in such high esteem. They remained humble and gracious to their acceptance as the people's expected saviors. Secretly they prayed that they could provide the redemption that the people sought.

They rode to where Black Wolf and his party had been hard at work. He was excited to see them! Tamara and Tobin were immediately taken back to the difficulty of their task and the progress that they had made. They had forgotten how steep the lower angle of the rock was. After all, it had been at night when they descended, and it seemed mild in comparison to what they had climbed to get there. Despite all of this, Black Wolf and his braves had amassed a huge amount of wood to the point where the horses could safely haul them without injury.

110

CHAPTER 44

Their difficulty was getting the wood reduced to the size where humans could move it the rest of the way up the rock. Tamara came up with a quick solution. She removed her backpack and produced a sling of climbing gear and a couple of climbing ropes. Tobin knew instantly where she was headed with this. This was her moment to shine, so he let her do her thing.

She gracefully ascended the rock taking a much more direct route than the braves who were engaged in hauling the wood. They all looked on, impressed by her bravery and skill. Within minutes she was on top of a ledge, fastening her anchors. She checked their security and then ran the ropes she was carrying through the carabiners. She had already tied the two ropes together using a figure eight. When the knot reached the apex where she was standing, she fed it through the carabiners so their lengths would be evenly matched. Satisfied that things were evenly matched and in proper order, she repelled back down to Tobin and Black Wolf. She then fashioned a slip knot to the wider end of one of the medium-sized logs. With the assistance of some of the younger braves they safely pulled the length of the wood to the ledge. This was much more expedient and would be even more so when they retrieved the harness used by Camaxtli tomorrow. They pulled a few more logs to the ledge and were delighted by the ease of the pulley system that Tamara had created.

From the rock to the ledge then to the top of the rock, they had an additional one hundred feet to gain. They would have to do it in a series with their limited gear. They would use Camaxtli to safely haul and stack as many logs as possible to the first ledge. From that point, they would need to move the anchors to the top of the rock and repeat the process without the assistance of Camaxtli. The day had grown long and it was time to return to the base camp before the light would fail them.

Red Bear, Tobin, Tamara, and Black Wolf held counsel that night. Red Bear pointed out that a new moon would appear in only a few days, increasing the chance appearance of the Skywalkers. No one wanted this. Tobin didn't want them to know about the work they had done. He doubted that they would know the purpose of it anyway, but he still preferred to have stealth on his side. They agreed to spend one more day in labor and return to the sanctuary of the cave the following day.

Tobin and Tamara were impressed by Red Bear and the warriors' progress at the ground site. Tobin instructed them to hide the gold foil near the sight and return to the safety of the sanctuary. At first, Red Bear protested. He wanted to stay and help his lord. Tobin explained that they had more than enough work to do on top of the rock in Black Wolf's party and to have more people in the way would be counterproductive. On top of that, it would be better for all if the parties were split into two groups in case an expedient escape was needed. Reluctantly Red Bear led his warriors back toward their sanctuary.

Tamara and Tobin retrieved the harness for Camaxtli and followed Red Bear to the split in the trail. They bade farewell and then road on to meet up with Black Wolf and his party. Upon arriving, they marveled at the progress that they had made. The ledge where Tamara had installed the pulley system was full. She didn't waste any time and quickly arranged for the proper pulley system to get the logs to the top. She was shocked to see how much timber they had already amassed. They wasted no time emptying the ledge and relocating the pulley system to repeat the process. They did this several times, and with the added help of the mighty Camaxtli, the work went quickly.

CHAPTER 45

Clouds had started to emerge a few hours before and it appeared as if it would rain at any moment. Black Wolf had already instructed the braves to return to the base camp while a small portion stayed to move the last load from the ledge to the top. Thirty minutes after they departed, the unmistakable sound of thundering hoofbeats could be heard coming up the mountain.

Tamara and Tobin stood atop the ledge at the intermittent point to the top. There were still several logs needing to be moved the remainder of the way. As the braves came into view, they could see the fear on their faces. They were being followed by what Tamara and Tobin now knew to be the Skywalkers, who appeared to be sliding across the ground rather than running. Tamara had an idea and instructed Tobin and the braves to gather behind the logs. Her intent was obvious. After the last rider had passed, they rolled the logs off of the ledge sending them crashing down toward the Skywalkers. It appeared as if it was a direct hit, but the logs passed through the Skywalkers without any effect on their progress.

They had the braves pinned at the end of the trail. They sat motionless upon their horses, surrounded by the Skywalkers. Tobin, Tamara, and Black Wolf stared on in horror when, all of a sudden, the braves and Skywalkers started to shimmer and then simply vanish, leaving their horses standing there, clearly confused and distraught. Tamara, Tobin, Black Wolf, and the remaining braves stood frozen with fear, not knowing what to do. They remained that way for several moments before huddling against the rock and discussing what to do. Moments later, they heard the braves on top, yelling and screaming. Then all was quiet again. Unanimously they decided to stay hidden on the ledge hoping that they would be obscured by their position. They sat there watching as a dark ship descended from the clouds and moved to the west till it vanished from sight. Only then did they descend to the horses and search for survivors.

Finding not a one they galloped to the base camp and the shelter of the cave. Each one praying for their friends' safety that had departed earlier in the day. Not knowing if the Skywalkers would circle back, they decided to stay at the base camp. They took turns being sentries so the others could rest. Sleep did not come easy for any of them as they kept replaying the day's events and wondering what had happened to their friends.

At dawn, under clear skies, they set out for the safety of the cavern. Some of the horses that had returned to the camp followed them while others did not. The five riders were too laden with the burden to care. They rode on in relative silence, scanning the sky and horizons for signs of peril. They rode the twenty miles to the corral without incident.

The braves watching over the corrals spoke with Black Wolf and told him that Red Bear and his party of seventy-some riders had arrived the day before without incident. One of the braves then went on to explain that riderless horses kept appearing throughout the night. He had sent word to Red Bear, who told him to give it a day to see if any of your party returned. If not, then he would dispatch a search party to go looking for them. The brave asked Black Wolf about the fate of the others. He explained that they were the only five who remained. The brave broke out in lamentations for his brother, who had been one of their party. Both Tamara's and Tobin's hearts sank.

Red Bear was grateful to see the arrival of Tobin, Tamara, Black Wolf, and the two warriors. He exclaimed, "Thanks to the Sky Father and Earth Mother, I feared all hope had been lost."

CHAPTER 46

The mood throughout the rest of the cavern was somber. They had not suffered a loss as great as this in many, many seasons. It was decided that they would not return until the end of this lunar cycle, for it was known that the Skywalkers always appear when it's a blood moon, and the next moon would be a blood moon.

The following day, they performed a ceremony to help their lost brethren pass onto the spirit world. As sad as the occasion was, it was a magical night of dancing and mysticism.

To know the people better who they were trying to help, Tamara and Tobin decided to meet with all of the families who had lost an immediate loved one due to the incident on top of Flat Top Rock. It seemed that consisted of most of the people who lived in the village. During the next few weeks, they drank in the culture, warmth, and hospitality of their hosts. They were now filled with a revived sense of purpose.

It was decided that only six warriors would accompany the foursome this time since 90 percent of the work was already complete. During their short reprieve, Tamara was presented with a fine longbow, which she relished as a prize since archery was one of her hobbies. Tobin was presented with a tunic weaved of finely meshed gold and beads. He also received a golden encrusted chest plate. It was of unparalleled quality, and Tobin was honored to wear it.

They had used their time well and fine-tuned the plan to optimize their efficiency upon the arrival of the Skywalkers. It was also decided that three braves would accompany Red Bear for the rolling of the gold foil at the base of the rock. The other three would accompany Black Wolf to finish off the bonfire pile that was nearly finished when they were attacked. Tamara and Tobin would repel to the top of the giant roof and would drill and place the pipe bombs. The party departed for Flat Top Rock twelve days before the blood moon would be full. Tobin felt much better about the shorter line of ten riders. It would be far easier for them to break and scatter than the last time. Hopefully, that wouldn't be necessary, but it was much better to be prepared than not.

Fortunately, their approach ride went off without a hitch. That afternoon they sat around a fire and ate fresh fish that they had caught from the creek at base camp. As usual, they extinguished their fire before nightfall, turning in early, weary from their travels.

At dawn, they ate a quick breakfast and headed straight to their designated work sites. Work went well for all parties. For Red Bear and his crew, the hardest part was getting the large rolls of gold into the bowl without damaging them. They used a horse with a sleigh-type gurney to lower the rolls into place before unrolling them. It worked well, and they completed their task before returning to camp.

Black Wolf and his crew worked well and efficiently together. The labor was tiresome, and by the time they were required to return to camp, they had assembled a cabin-style structure that reached two stories in height and could be seen from ten miles or more. Tobin and Tamara were confronted by a different circumstance altogether. Upon repelling to the roof, they found it to be about twenty feet larger than they had remembered it. Tamara said, "Well, it just goes to figure that this is the past and we haven't detonated the explosives that shortened the roof yet."

Tobin said, "That's a good sign. It means that it must have worked!"

Tamara replied, "Or might not have and just occurred naturally over time. You can clearly see a fissure running the length of the roof."

"That's good too," said Tobin, "less drilling." He showed Tamara where he wanted to place the charges and gave her the drill.

CHAPTER 47

He used his water bag to make a drip system to keep the bit from overheating and rendering it useless. While Tamara concentrated on making the holes, Tobin went to fabricating the explosives. Having the natural fissure there was a huge help and a good sign. It showed where the sediment in granite had cooled at different temperatures when it formed the roof, thus creating a weak spot in it. Things were moving along faster than expected all the way around. Tamara had finished drilling the last hole about the same time Tobin completed the last pipe bomb. She asked, "Do you think this will work?"

He told her, "We'll find out soon enough. But I'm confident it will!" Tobin produced a large ziplock bag and placed the pipe bombs inside. He then wrapped them in another bag and hid them in the fissure. They then climbed to the top where they met up with Black Wolf and his team and rode back to base camp together.

Upon reaching base camp, they fell into conversation with Red Bear. They were pleased to find out that everything was completed and in place all around. The only thing that was left for Tobin and Tamara to do was to place the charges and run the fuse. After dinner, they extinguished the fire and were returning to the shelter of the cave when Tamara stopped to stare at the sky. She clasped Tobin on the shoulder telling him, "Look! It's the aurora borealis."

He was in the middle of explaining how they were too far south for it to be the lights of the aurora borealis when the sky started to shimmer then all went black.

They were mostly sheltered by the cave at this point when the Skywalkers' ship appeared as if out of nowhere. It was so large it blocked most of the stars from their vision. With the exception of an occasional vacuuming sound, it was utterly silent. The ship was entirely black except for squares at the top and a few lights at its center. Tobin assumed the boxes at the top were some kind of viewing portals while the ones at its side were running lights. The ship was huge and shaped like a Doritos tortilla chip, and the sheer mass of it diminished his spirit, but he wouldn't let the others see it. He stood just outside the entrance as if in a show of defiance in the face of a deadly foe. The rest watched from the shelter of the cave until the ship disappeared in the western sky.

They took turns as sentries that night. Sleep did not come easily. The upside was that they knew the Skywalkers were out there somewhere, but where? Tobin spent many hours during the night, making a fuse out of hemp rope and bat guano. When he was finished, he had nearly thirty feet of fuse.

That morning, after breakfast, they decided on a plan that would help keep Tamara and Tobin in the know since they both needed to be close to the blast area to ignite the fuse. Their view would be limited to the northwest sky as this was the side of the rock that the roof laid on. To help counter this they would send two scouts to opposite sides of their position. Two to the east and two to the south. Obviously, the most unencumbered view would be from the top of Flat Top Rock, but the fire at the top would be so massive and generate so much heat that no one would be able to be posted there. That was okay. They did not need a scout above them. Because of its massive size, the ship would be plainly obvious when it was upon them. If the ship appeared in the southern sky, that scout would ignite a signal fire or vice versa if it was spotted in the east. This way they would know what direction the ship would approach from. When the ship was close to the central location, the second scout would light his fire. Therefore, when they saw two fires in the distance, they would know that the time to ignite the fuse was close at hand.

CHAPTER 48

After the fires were lit, they were to meet up with Red Bear and his cohorts at the base camp. Black Wolf and his brave would accompany Tobin and Tamara to the top of the rock. After Tamara and Tobin repelled into position, placed the charges and the fuse, and found a safe location to witness the blast, Black Wolf and his cohort would wait till dusk or upon the sight of the Skywalkers and ignite the fire atop of the rock. Thus, with the plan established, they rode out to their designated posts to watch and wait.

Tamara and Tobin had to make two double-rope repels to get into a good position to ignite the fuse while still having communication with the top. Once the fuse was lit by Tobin, he would have to make a pendulum motion running back and forth while attached to the climbing rope until he reached the proper height of the ledge from where he and Tamara would watch while still being sheltered from the blast.

There were a few scattered clouds that morning. The air was crisp and the temperature mild. They had been trapped for nearly five months now in the past. While Tobin longed to free his people, he longed to be home as well. He wondered if he and Tamara had been written off for dead and if any deals had been struck during their absence. He could only hope for the best. Tobin wired the fuses into the pipe bombs while Tamara placed the bombs into their allotted spots and sealed the holes with wax to prevent moisture from damaging them. Tamara was trying to place the last charge when a mouse came running out of the hole. It scurried across the rock only to be snatched up by an owl that seemed to appear out of nowhere and then just flew off. Tobin didn't know what to make of it. Tamara just said, "Wow, that's strange!"

Everything was set now, and they just waited for the appearance of the Skywalkers. They sat atop the ledge chatting and waiting for the signal. Tobin would have to leave the ledge to ignite the fuse even with the thirty feet of fuse he had made. After wiring the explosives to go off at approximately the same time, it left him with only seven feet of slack. Timing was everything, and he wanted to be precise. The clouds had slowly built throughout the day. He and Tamara could only hope for the best, and they were both startled by a war cry from above that announced the lighting of the fire.

Soon after that, they saw the signal fire in the east spring to life. They both felt butterflies in their stomachs. Tobin swung into position and waited as he felt a spot of rain hit his forehead. Silently he said a prayer, "Please, God, don't rain now." As soon as he finished his prayer, the signal fire from the south sprung to life. He knew the time was close, yet he waited telling himself that timing was everything. He would have roughly ten minutes to swing himself to the safety of the ledge after lighting the fuse. He purposely placed the fuse below him so his movement wouldn't affect the fuse. To light it, he was practically upside down dangling from the rock.

The tip of the ship appeared above him. He judged its speed and lit the fuse. It took him four swings to reach the safety of the ledge where he and Tamara watched as stars disappeared from view. Eagerly they watched the fuse burn toward the detonators. All looked well. The fuse burned to the critical point where it split into the individual charges. There were five charges altogether. The two charges farthest from them were run on the same fuse and were closer together than the other charges. Tobin watched and his heart sank as the fuse to those charges fizzled and stopped. The slight sprinkle of rain must have dampened the fuse. Tamara looked to Tobin and asked with alarm in her voice, "Will three charges work?"

"I'm not sure," Tobin replied.

CHAPTER 49

She produced her bow and quivered an arrow, took aim, and let it fly! A spark lighted the rock a little more than an inch above the fuse. She quickly quivered another and let it rip. She was dead on and the fuse sprung to life. She looked at Tobin, explaining, "Flint-rock tips!"

Tobin just looked at her amazed and exclaimed, "I love you, woman!"

The blast went off like clockwork. The ship now covered the night sky. A large portion of the rock's roof went crashing to the valley floor. A magnetic pulse would be neither seen nor heard. The two lovers stood holding each other in suspense. It seemed like a lifetime, but Tobin knew it could only have been seconds before the running lights went dark and the swishing sound stopped. The massive ship appeared to stop its forward progress and lurch backward as much like a Frisbee did when it lost its spin. The ship was coming down—straight down!

They could hear metal crashing against rock and they needed to find shelter fast. Tobin looked to where the massive roof had just split in two and saw that there was still a large roof remaining. He grabbed Tamara, exclaiming, "Make for the roof!" They were anchored to the same rope, and as a single unit, they swung for the shelter. They were going to make it as metal and rock came raining down all around them. They were almost there when Tobin saw a shimmer in the air before them. They swung into the safety of the roof and all went quiet. There was no longer the sound of crashing metal against rock. The shower of flame logs and loose rubble simply ceased.

The two climbers sat there trying to gain their wits. Tamara was the first to speak, asking, "What's happening?"

"I think we shifted again" Tobin answered.

"What about Black Wolf and Red Bear?" she inquired.

He said, "I guess we'll never know."

Tamara looked toward the valley. "Oh my word! We're definitely not home, are we?" she replied.

The valley where the reservation that they had lived in was now an ocean of lights. Looking to the sky, only a third of the stars in the night sky were visible. They knew that it was due to light pollution. Off in the distance, they could see rivers of red and white lights. Tobin attributed that to freeway traffic. The meadow that contained the hangar and airstrip now housed vast structures of an odd architectural style. What really caught their attention was the massive amounts of air traffic crisscrossing across the sky. The two of them sat there hanging in their harnesses for quite some time taking in their new surroundings.

They decided after a short deliberation to climb to the top of the remaining rock and make their way toward civilization. They were just reaching the top of Flat Top Rock, which was now how they remembered it from their time zone, when a loud bomb-like warning horn started to blare. Spotlights from the structures in the meadow started to sweep the landscape. Tobin and Tamara had no idea what was going on, but somehow inwardly they knew it was about them. Out of nowhere, they heard a loud cry, "Tobin and Tamara, come over here. Quickly!" They weren't sure who the voice was calling to. It sounded out again, "Tobin, Tamara, over here. Quickly, we must get going!"

At the bottom of the low-angled slab, they could make out a silhouette of a large man. "Quickly now! We have to hurry!"

They made their way to the large figure, and he said, "Follow me. It won't take them long to pinpoint our location."

Tobin asked, "Who is *them*, and why are they after us?"

"Why the Trilateral Group, of course. First, because you're alien citizens, and second because you brought down their slave craft. You're in much danger, and we must be going!"

They followed him down the valley to a small craft. Tobin didn't notice it at first, but as they approached, he saw no road and noticed that the vehicle hovered slightly above the ground. They quickly got into the vehicle.

CHAPTER 50

As they sat on the seats, straps sprang from behind them, crossing their chests and securing them to their seats. The driver wasted no time as they sped off just above the treetops. The vehicle was moving at an incredible rate of speed and was amazingly agile. Despite its speed and rapid motion, the ride was surprisingly smooth. It was as if the seats were somehow suspended in the air and the vehicle was rotating around them.

Tobin thought what amazing technology. Tamara was speechless. She looked at the two men. It appeared as if they were looking at their reflection in a mirror with one being older than the other. They'd been in such a hurry to exit the area that Tobin hadn't yet even looked at the man who had come to their aid. When he finally did his heart, skipped a beat, and he yelled, "Dad!" Tears were welling in his eyes and he could barely contain his emotions.

"Yes, Tobin. I've been trying to reach you for twenty years, but I knew I could reach you now at this time. I've been longing for this moment for a very long time. I will explain everything to you once we get you two somewhere safe."

As they reached the city district, Tobin was astounded by what he saw. Vehicles were flying through the air, going to and fro in a very orderly fashion. The buildings were of an amazing height and design. He could see people milling around on the sidewalks along with land-roving vehicles filling the streets. They approached a midsized building when the vehicle turned vertical and a door appeared with a conveyor line of cars inside. Their car slid into a vacant slot. Their seats had already spun around allowing them to sit upright. The door slid open, and stairs slid out to their adjusted heights. They exited the vehicle, and it vanished in a seemingly endless line of other vehicles.

They entered a lobby, got into an elevator as Tobin's father instructed it to which apartment he wanted to go to. His eyes were scanned and they were swiftly ushered to his apartment, moving both horizontally and vertically. Tamara asked, "What year is this?"

Tobin's father explained "2086." It was a modest apartment, sparsely furnished. "Come in and sit down. Are you thirsty or hungry?" Tobin's father asked.

Tobin asked for a beer and Tamara opted for water.

"How is your mother, Tobin?" he asked.

"She is devastated that you abandoned us," Tobin replied.

"It's not that simple, son. Like the two of you, I had no clue what I was getting into when I visited the sacred lands. I've jumped time twenty-six times trying to get back to you and your mother. Every time it's different, and I even got close once. The problem was that I hadn't gone missing yet and not knowing the ramifications of running into myself, I didn't make contact."

"How did you know to come to our aid tonight?" Tamara asked.

"I made a time jump two years ago to tomorrow's date. You can imagine my shock when I saw my son and you, Tamara, had been captured. I made a jump and two years prior till today was the closest I had ever come, so I waited," he answered.

"Why were we captured?" asked Tobin.

His father explained, "You made some very important people in high places very upset when you brought down their slave ship."

"Slave ship?" Tamara asked.

"Yes. I'll elaborate, but it will take a while. Are you sure you're not hungry?" he inquired.

Tobin replied, "Actually, yes, I could eat something."

Tamara also said that she was hungry too.

"What would you like to eat, Tamara?" he asked.

She jokingly said, "Mahi-mahi with crab-stuffed mushrooms and a mai tai." She was startled when a cylinder-shaped object projected up from the floor with a covered plate on top of it and a mai tai next to it. "Now that's service!" she exclaimed.

Tobin was amazed but wasted no time ordering. "I'd like a T-bone steak, medium rare, baked stuffed potato, and a Sierra Nevada Pale Ale."

Once they were eating, Tobin's father went on to explain how the world currently came into being.

CHAPTER 51

"In the year 2023, because of global warming, a large section of the polar ice cap went crashing into the Atlantic Ocean. It created a tidal wave over three miles high, and a third of the world's population was wiped away within six hours of the polar slide. As the oceans cooled, it kicked in another ice age, further reducing the earth's population. Crops vanished, and disease ran rampant, leaving only the extremely wealthy and extremely well prepared to survive. The ten richest families remaining on earth formed a pack. The new world could not maintain the numbers from before the disasters, and neither did they desire such a large population in the future. An elixir was developed from a mineral substance that was mined from our lands. This elixir stopped the aging process and cured all diseases. Its only side effect is that it rendered its consumer impotent.

"The ten elders of each family agreed to provide the serum to their family members once they reached the mature age of forty. While other families struggled for food and survival, these families flourished. Their only problem becoming greed and luxury. With the workforce becoming diminished and the world on the mend, they needed more laborers. Their scientists learned how to manipulate the earth's magnetic field to bend or shorten and lengthen time. By doing this and somehow using the gravitational pull of the moon, they were able to build a ship that could jump in time."

Tobin interjected, "That's the reason all the ancient monuments are built to track the sun and moon!"

"Exactly," his father exclaimed. "In fact, years used to be measured on a lunar scale, not solar!"

Tamara asked, "What's the moon got to do with all this?"

Tobin's father said, "I'm not exactly sure, but I believe that it's something to do with the time shift."

Tobin chimed in. "I have a theory. The moon controls the tides, and humans are ninety percent water. I think the lunar pull on water has the same effect on our bodies. That combined with the magnetic field of the earth must open a portal in space-time at areas of high magnetic fluctuation or areas of potential energy such as the roof on Flat Top Rock."

Tamara and Tobin's father both nodded their heads in agreement.

"I think you're onto something," Tobin's father said.

"That has to be the reason the ancients constructed such grand and astronomically correct structures all over the planet that correlate with the earth's ley lines and magnetic fields," Tobin said.

"It does help explain the disappearance of large civilizations of people for no apparent reason," Tamara thoughtfully said.

"We're definitely on the right track," Tobin's father said.

Tobin asked, "What's this slave ship business all about?"

Tobin's father answered, "As I was saying, there was a vast shortage of laborers to cater to the whims of these overly lavish families. So they went back in time and brought people from the past. They wipe out their memories and implant new ones. They spay them like they are pets and put them down if one of them falls ill."

"That's awful! How can they morally justify this in their minds?" asked Tamara.

"They reason that they're saving them from a miserable death brought on by the American Indian wars. The aftermath, such as the Trail of Tears and the diseases that followed." He told her.

"That's insane! They're stealing our people's souls, identities, and lives!" Tobin exclaimed.

"Now you know why I had to be here when you appeared. You caused huge damage to their operation. That was their only ship, and it will take years for them to construct another one. More importantly, if we can get you back to stop the leasing of our lands, especially to the mining company, which is a subsidiary of the Trilateral Group, you can change this future, son. We need to get you and Tamara back to your time. We just have to figure out how to do that," Tobin's father stated.

CHAPTER 52

"I've developed a theory about that. As I said earlier, our bodies being ninety percent water. The moon must somehow have a pull on our bodies. We were climbing relatively close to the autumn equinox in our time under a waning moon. *Waning* being the keyword here, the moon was diminishing on its regressive phase, hence moving backward in time. Maybe, and it's a big maybe, if we were to be climbing in roughly the same place at roughly the same time during the vernal equinox, which is the polar opposite of the autumn equinox during the waxing moon, we could possibly move back to our own time," Tobin speculated.

"I don't know. That's a big stretch," said Tamara.

Tobin's father replied, "That may sound a bit fanciful, but in autumn things are in regression, and in spring things are in bloom. It's no coincidence that the ancients built such elaborate solar and lunar dials."

"I suppose the position of the earth will determine where in the universe we end up, huh?" asked Tamara.

"I don't know, Tamara. I said it's just a theory. Before all of this the thought of time travel was absurd to both of us!" said Tobin.

"That's an understatement!" exclaimed Tamara.

Tobin's father speculated, "I think your theory holds some plausibility. Besides, it's the only theory we have and we're close to the vernal equinox. They'll be looking for the two of you, and I can't conceal you for very long. I am of the slave class, and they do random searches of my class and you're not marked." He then revealed a tattoo on his wrist. "All citizens receive a mark."

"I have so many questions. What's up with these Skywalker monsters?" asked Tobin.

His father told him, "They're holograms designed to freeze their victims in terror. Then they'd lock onto them and teleport them onto the slave ship. It's very effective and noninvasive as they so arrogantly put it."

Tobin said, "So that's why the logs rolled right through them!"

Tamara chimed in, "They are terrifying! I froze at the first sight of them. It is a very effective tactic."

Tobin's father said, "Once they're on the ship they are so thrilled to be greeted by people and disoriented by what's happened to them they're easily manipulated. So I'm told."

"That's awful," Tamara sadly stated.

"It only gets worse from there. Families are separated. Men and women get sterilized. Their memories are erased and replaced with new ones and then they get sent to their new owners where they'll work for room and board till they get either ill or are no longer useful. Then they will be put down just like animals. The two of you can stop all of this. That's why I waited all this time for you! For now, you must be exhausted. Let me show you to your room," stated Tobin's father.

The room was cozy, meaning small, but had all that they needed, including a full bath and a garment maker, complete with a catalog of items it could make. They showered, made passionate love, and fell asleep in each other's embrace. Tobin woke during the night. Something was troubling him about his theory. His theory made sense only if they were to make the jump from the time they had just departed, not the one they arrived in! This put a whole new twist on things. He wondered if they'd have to make two jumps to get to their time using the polar opposite of where they were now and from where they had just left. Then do the same from that time to the time they originally disappeared from. The other possibility being, to take the time that they had just come from to the time they were now in, total it, then divide it by their original time and then adjust it to the lunar cycle. Being somewhat of a mathematician, he decided on the latter.

CHAPTER 53

He spent the rest of the night doing the math and studying the lunar cycles for regularity. What he finally decided was that they needed to jump in two days from now at ten o'clock at night. Whether it was pure coincidence or fate, Tobin could not determine. He preferred the latter to the former. When Tamara awoke, he told her of his findings. She still thought it a little far-fetched, but it was better than no theory at all, which was what she had.

He explained his finding to his father and they made plans to be in the right place at the right time. It's funny how difficult a simple task should be and this was no exception to the rule. Tobin's father told Tobin and Tamara that the sacred tribal lands were now owned by the Trilateral Group and that gaining access was difficult and highly dangerous but not impossible. He told them that he would make arrangements to accomplish their goal.

Some specialty items would be required. To get them where they needed to be would be another issue, and Tobin's father knew just the person to help. He was a scientist that worked for the Trilateral Group. Although he was an immortal, he didn't agree with the use of humans being treated in such an inhumane way.

They were going to need thermal underwear that would hide their heat signature. The grounds all around the Trilateral building were teeming with heat monitors and security personnel. Tobin's father knew he could get them there. After all, he got them out of there, but this time the circumstances were quite different. At the time of their escape, they were dealing with the subsequent crash of the slave ship for cover. Now they would be on high alert, thinking it would be an inside job or system malfunction that caused the slave ship to crash. This thought prompted Tobin's father to ask how they accomplished that daunting task in the remote past.

Tobin explained how they were met by Black Wolf and his braves when he killed the deer. Then how he met Red Bear, who was now the medicine man for the tribe, and how they had gathered gold because of the instruction that his father had given to Red Bear as a child. Tobin's father was amazed by the tale and about the completion of the escape route from the cave. He told Tobin and Tamara that he had instructed them to acquire the gold for wealth and was pleased to hear that it was used for a much more noble cause. Tamara exclaimed how amazingly fun the escape slide was and how sweetly Moon Song, who was Red Bear's mother, had treated them. She explained how weird she felt being treated as a god. Tobin's father understood very well where she was coming from. He had come to know and care for them as his own. He was well pleased to hear of their prosperity and knew they would be celebrating their freedom from the Skywalkers.

After retrieving the necessary supplies, they returned to his father's apartment and talked well into the night. Tobin's father explained how he had tried to get back to his own time, but he never realized the importance of the lunar pull. He told them how he affected the future by changing past actions, sometimes for the better, sometimes for the worse. But it all took a toll on his psyche.

Tobin and Tamara slept most of the next day while his father was at work. It had been a crazy chain of events that he and Tamara had endured together. He had truly come to admire her wit, charm, courage, and beauty. He had fallen head over heels in love with her and fallen hard. Tobin's father returned at six in the evening.

CHAPTER 54

They enjoyed dinner together and departed his father's apartment at eight o'clock. They took the highway up the Owens River Valley, exiting at Lone Pine. From there they went off the road, skirting the treetops of the valley behind Flat Top Rock, keeping under the radar systems of the Trilateral Group. The plan was simple. They dump the vehicle in the valley then hike up the backside of Flat Top Rock to avoid detection. Once there, they would climb the low angle slab to the top, and from there they would do two double-rope repels to get them in position under the roof. At approximately 9:45, they would ascend the roof and if Tobin was right, they would climb through a time vortex back to their own time.

The threesome ditched the car and were donning their gear when they were startled by the sound of a rustling in the woods behind them. A large bull elk emerged and stood there watching them for a moment and walked off. Tobin's father exclaimed, "How extraordinary! Elk were thought to be extinct from this region years ago." This prompted Tobin to ask his father if he knew the significance of sighting an elk, an owl, and a mouse would be. Tobin's father asked, "All at the same time?"

"A very close proximity," answered Tobin.

"Let me chew on that while we hike," his father answered.

They moved on in relative silence, each lost in his private thoughts. Upon arriving atop the rock, they set their anchors and repelled into place. They needed to perform a little upclimbing to get under the roof. All of these tasks would have been impossible without the night vision goggles that his father's friend had provided. The time had come and Tobin began his ascension of the awesome roof. Tobin's father was impressed with his son's climbing skills. Tobin and

Tamara had been intent on the task at hand and hadn't been paying attention to his father. If they would have, they'd have noticed him putting on a skydiving pack and disengaging from the climbing gear.

All of a sudden, a siren was heard coming from the compound below, followed by spotlights sweeping the rock and canyons below. Tobin's father yelled to the both of them, "Finish what you started, and change this future!"

Tobin looked to his father, saying, "You're coming with us. I'm not leaving you!"

Then his father said, "It's not my destiny. It's yours! Mine is to distract them so you and Tamara can complete yours. I know the meaning!" With that, he turned and leaped from the rock!

Tobin and Tamara stared in horror and shock. A huge sigh of relief washed over them when they saw the parachute deploy. Tamara yelled to Tobin, "What should we do?"

He just kept climbing and said, "Finish what we started." He noticed as he kept climbing that the sound of the siren had diminished. He completed the roof and put Tamara on belay. He could no longer see the spotlights. Tamara climbed with a newfound zeal and joined him within minutes. By the time they arrived at the top of the rock, they could no longer hear the sirens.

As soon as they cleared the roof, the giant structure of the Trilateral Group had vanished from sight. They were certain that they had jumped in time. Now they just hoped Tobin had calculated correctly. They ascended to the top of the rock. It was flat. That was a good start for sure! They climbed down the back of the low-angle slab and headed in the direction of their original base camp. They passed the area where they had slept the second night of their adventure.

It was the sight that had once served as a tepee site in the far-distant past. There was no sign that a recent fire had ever burned there. That was another welcomed sign.

CHAPTER 55

What really set their hearts ablaze was when they reached the knoll that their tent rested on and there it sat. There were no signs of their horses' tracks running toward the valley. They embraced each other and Tamara whispered into Tobin's ear, "You did it, Tobin!"

He replied, "Let's not count our chickens just yet!"

They took time to refresh themselves and break down their camp. After they stashed their saddles, they made their way down the game trail toward their truck. When they reached the place where they could clearly see their truck, their hearts leaped again. It was a trifecta of good signs. There was no sight of Camaxtli or Atlauva and they didn't expect there to be as they weren't with them when they made the jump in time.

Tobin fetched his keys from the horse trailer fender and jumped into the truck. It fired up right away. Tamara took her phone from her backpack and plugged it into the truck. She gave it a few minutes then turned it on. Looking at Tobin, she said, "According to the phone, we've been only gone one day!"

Tobin replied, "It's been one helluva a long day!"

Tamara asked, "What should we do about the horses?"

He answered, "There's not much we can do. Besides, they're in good hands, and who knows they might just change history! Remember the pact we made as kids. That was the whole reason we named our horses after the Aztec gods."

Tamara said, "I don't know about you, but I'm homesick. I could use a shower and some fresh clothes."

"That sounds like a winner!" Tobin said as they started for the stables.

"What do you want to tell the tribal council, Tobin?" she asked.

"Let's start with anything but the truth. Who in their right mind would believe us if we did? I think we should take a couple of days to write our reports then get together and make sure they're somewhat copacetic. Then we'll submit them to the council for review. The council meeting for the vote is a week from today. I'll meet you in your office with my recommendation and report in two days," he said. Then he kissed her goodbye as he dropped her off at her suburban. He then dropped off the horse trailer and headed home.

Two days later, they met at Tamara's office to fine-tune their findings and opinions on the land leasing. Satisfied, their reports were varied enough to make it look like they didn't collaborate yet sufficient enough to show reason not to lease their sacred lands. They drove separate vehicles to the town hall and dropped off the research findings for the council. Then they returned to Tamara's house where they reminisced about their adventure and made sweet love.

It appeared as if the whole reservation showed up for the vote on leasing the tribal sacred lands. Tobin and Tamara had no way of knowing that another council member and another one's wife had fallen sick. Despite their reports, the council voted six to four in favor of leasing the land.

Tobin and Tamara were beside themselves with grief. As they were leaving the meeting, the tribal chief approached them. "I'm sorry. I know from your reports how you both feel about leasing the sacred lands. The fact is people no longer care for the past or the things that mattered to our elders. They only see the good. A new school and medical center will provide for our people."

CHAPTER 56

"Tobin, your father gave me this to give to you at a troubling time such as this! He told me that I would know the time, and this feels like the time. I had asked him where he had gone and why he didn't give it to you himself. He just handed me this envelope and said you'd understand. Again, I'm sorry for the council's decision, but unless we can find the funding elsewhere in two weeks from today, the deal will be finalized." He bid them farewell and left.

Tamara said, "Open the envelope."

He did, and inside was a picture showing an owl swooping down to catch the mouse for his dinner. An elk was standing with its back end over the mouse. The elk spotted the owl's move to attack, so he crapped on the mouse. The mouse stood there with one paw in the air, giving the owl the finger and the other holding up a gold nugget. The owl, now seeing the mouse covered in shit, decided he'd seek dinner elsewhere and flew off.

> The meaning of the elk, the owl, and the mouse is that not everyone who shits on you means harm.

> Love,
> Dad

PS: Remember the gold.

Tamara faced Tobin, and they simultaneously said to each other, "The gold! There's our funding!"

Here is an excerpt from the second book in the Shimmer Series "Hell or High Water"

HELL OR HIGH WATER

Tobin's father, Wyllie, had prepared for a worst case. He knew it might be necessary to create a diversion that would allow Tobin and Tamara to get through the time portal. Considering that the portal was more than two thousand feet up the side of a vertical granite rock mountain, he surmised that a parachute would allow him to separate himself from Tamara and Tobin in a quick fashion, creating an ample diversion to occupy the security personnel of the Trilateral Group. Following someone sailing through the night sky under a twenty-seven-by-six-foot parachute would be enough to grab their attention and keep it. Tracking the parachute as it sailed through the dark evening sky would most definitely keep the attention of the security personnel and spotlights that have been strategically placed around the grounds of the time traveling slave ships enterprise.

The slave ships were designed by the Trilateral Group and their immortal board, which was made up of self-proclaimed royalty. The sad part was the fact that they were using the people that they abducted from their own time and brought to theirs to protect the very same facility that enslaved them to begin with. Not only was it a sadly ironic state of affairs, but it was quite common of the human race, thought Wyllie as the searchlights scoured the night sky, trying to keep track of him. He crisscrossed the sky, turning left or right and going into stalls or dives any time one of the lights locked on to him. Wyllie had definitely taken all the attention away from Tobin and Tamara, who would have been difficult to spot even if the light had managed to stop on them at that height. Positioned under the large roof as they climbed, they would have appeared as a mere speck on the wall, wholly undefinable without the aid of binoculars or infrared heat optics. Wyllie had given Tobin and Tamara all the time they would have required to make it through the portal back to the past.

It would be up to them with their newly acquired gift of knowledge to navigate the existence of time and space that he was flying through now. Nonetheless, Wyllie had no desire to be caught and detained. He was completely unsure of the consequences that could result from being trapped in a time that ceased to exist. What would be the ramifications if he disappeared? Would Tobin have ever been born? He reasoned that since it was the past, of course, he would have. Besides, if they were successful, he would have never been there to begin with. *Yet here I am. Does that indicate they failed?* he wondered. Was all of this work and planning for nothing? *Of course, not. Preposterous,* he thought as he was coming close to the tree line, skimming the tops of the trees close to the landing zone he picked days before just in case of an event such as this.

He rode by horseback to scout the terrain after hearing Tobin's theory of time portals, electromagnetic fields, and polarities. He managed to evade the security personnel and avoid triggering the heat and motion sensors that surrounded the property. He then hobbled his horse to a meadow not far from the clearing he designated to reconnect with the earth at. He was amazed at all the thoughts that could pass between his ears in such a short and adrenaline-filled descent from the cliff. With any luck, he'd escape capture and detainment. Then he would figure out how to extract himself from the period of time he hoped would have never existed. *If it never existed, how could I possibly be here? Could this be some kind of a really long semirealistic dream? Fuck! Quit thinking of probabilities and get away!* Wyllie could hear air bikes and see lights sweeping the hillside in their search for him. He quickly gathered his parachute and hid it under a nearby log. Using the trees for cover, he ran toward the meadow. There in the middle of the meadow stood his ride, chewing the grass that was richest in nutrients along the stream's edges. The moonlight sparkled off the gently rolling stream that wound through the open space, looking like a diamond snake slithering downhill. Wyllie didn't want to risk exposing his position by running in the open meadow. Time was of the essence. He still had five miles to go before reaching his car on the south side of the canyon. Deciding the risk was worth the time he would gain in exiting the region, he went for it.

ABOUT THE AUTHOR

James Sorenson was born in Panorama City, California. His mother, Sharon, and his father, Jim, moved the family to June Lake, California, when he was a young boy. There he learned to love and respect the magnificence of the world around him. He is an avid skier, rock climber, and all-around adventure seeker. Fascinated by the movement of the cosmos and our interconnectedness with the universe as a whole. He wrote a sports column for the *Mono Herald Review* and won the Best of Writers from the *Mammoth Times*. During his life, he experienced a career-ending accident as a professional skier. Not wanting to be tempted nor tortured by being surrounded by the beauty of the sierras and the awesome terrain it offers, he moved to Florida. There he owned a successful construction company and enjoyed margaritas on the beautiful white-sand beaches. After selling his company, he moved to Shreveport, Louisiana, where he enjoyed the variety of life in the swamplands, which landed him in jail. He escaped the corrupt state of Louisiana and is currently living on a river in the beautiful state of Oregon, where he enjoys teaching people in the arts of skiing and rock climbing, and the value of being good stewards to our mother planet. This is his first novel of a trilogy, which was written while he was incarcerated. He is currently working on the next book in this series titled *Hell or High Water*. He enjoys volunteering at the local food bank and looks forward to a more unified world, where love and peace prevail.